HEADQUARTERS

A BUILD Series Novel

C. ATKINSON

Copyright © 2023 by Charlene Akinson.

All rights reserved. No part of this book may be used or reproduced in any form whatsoever without written permission except in the case of brief quotations in critical articles or reviews.

This book is a work of fiction. Names, characters, businesses, organizations, places, events, and incidents either are the product of the author's imagination or are used fictitiously. Any resemblance to actual persons, living or dead, events, or locales is entirely coincidental.

Printed in the United States of America.

Book and cover design by JETLAUNCH

ISBN: 979-8-89079-104-7 (Paperback)
ISBN: 979-8-89079-105-4 (Hardcover)

First Edition: Month 2022

ALSO BY C. ATKINSON

The Build Series

Hard Hat

The Country Club

1

HEADQUARTERS. IT IS such an official title for a place. It's just a building—an office—that a company leases. Then, suddenly, it is the headquarters. It's like the cockpit of a jet, the driver's seat of a car, or the bridge of a ship.

The executives of the company work at headquarters. The accountants of the company work at headquarters. The estimating and business development staff work at headquarters.

Loretta Novak is thinking about what it will be like working at headquarters during her commute into the City. This is my first day back after the successful opening of the country club. *Who will I report to? What will I be responsible for? Where will I park my car?*

I pull into the parking garage below the building. Rich signals for me to stop and walks to my window.

"How are you, Loretta?"

"Fine, thanks,"

"Long time no see,"

"Well, I'm back here, working at headquarters until I get a new project to work on," I say.

"I always have room for your little Miata,"

"Thanks, Rich," I smile.

I walk around to the lobby and into the elevator. When the elevator arrives at the eleventh floor, I exit and head to Hank's office. He's probably the only one who knows I'm here. I knock on the door of Hank's office. Hank looks up and smiles at me.

"Come on in, Lolly," Hank says. "Take a seat. I'm glad you're here. We're a little short on work right now, so we can use your expertise in the estimating department. Let's go, and I'll introduce you to the chief estimator, Jose Animar. You can get acquainted with him and talk with him about what he wants you to do," Hank explains.

We leave Hank's office and walk down the hall to another corner office. Hank knocks, and we both walk in.

"Hi, Jose. Let me introduce you to Loretta Novak. She was the project manager on the country club project, and we have nowhere to put her right now. I figured estimating needs all hands on deck to pick up some new work,"

Jose stands and extends his hand to me. "Nice to meet you," Jose is an average-height, sort-of-round, and balding guy, probably in his forties. I noticed a picture of a small child in his office. I shake his hand and say, "Likewise."

"You can have the office next to mine. Go ahead and get settled. We have a weekly estimating and BD meeting in thirty minutes," Jose explains.

"What is BD?" I ask.

"Business development," Jose answers. "The meeting is in the bid room, right across the hall."

Hank and I start to leave Jose's office, and I say, "Thank you, both, for your time today. Hank, I'll stop by your office later," and walk into my new office.

I sit down and look around. My window looks right into the neighboring building across the alley—so much for a bay view. I take a few files out of my briefcase. It looks like they set me up with paper tablets, pens, and Post-it notes. I plug in my computer to see if I can access the corporate network. I get the circle of doom trying to boot up but realize I have to go to this meeting. My computer will have to wait.

I walk across the hall into the bid room. Jose is already getting ready as two others wander in. Another guy shows up and heads straight to the breakfast buffet. I jump in behind him and get a coffee and a chocolate donut. I turn and sit next to Hank. All the others file in behind me, grabbing some coffee and a snack. Once everyone is seated, Jose clears his throat.

"Good morning. Happy Monday. We have a newcomer to estimating from the field. This is Loretta Novak. You know Hank," Jose says to me, "but let me introduce you to the others in the room." Looking at the gal sitting across the table, Jose says, "This is Kathy Sullivan. She is our business development manager."

I look at her and smile.

"Dan Roberts is the operations manager of our structural group."

"Hi, Dan," I say.

"We have the Coral Towers bid coming up next week. I'm going to assign Loretta to take the lead on this one. It's mid-rise, twin towers, slab on grade with surface parking and landscaping," Jose describes.

"We really need to go after this project. The owner, Centurion Development, has a large portfolio, and if we are successful with this one, it could lead to more work," Kathy explains.

"What's the value of Coral Towers?" I ask.

"The engineer's estimate is $30 million," Kathy says.

"Do you need any more help with the bid?" Hank asks.

"I'll need three to analyze the subs' bids as they come in on bid day, which is a week from Thursday."

"I'll get some of my guys to help," Hank states.

"Me, too," Dan says. "My guys usually like coming to headquarters for a big bid."

"Great," Jose smiles. "Anyone else have anything we need to talk about?

"I have a qualification statement due on Friday for the San Francisco Zoo. I will need some help on this one," Kathy states.

"I'm having lunch with Mike Mathews from Delta Airlines," Dan interjects. "There is definitely potential work at the facility at SFO, which houses a large reservation center and an aircraft warehouse."

"I'm working with Goldman Sachs to negotiate a lease at One Sansome," Hank reveals. "They want to take the top three floors, the floors with the balconies."

"Are you working with Bob Kraft at One Sansome?" Kathy asks.

"Yeah, he's sort of a dud, but I don't have a choice," Hank admits. "That's why I'm talking directly to Goldman Sachs."

"Bob Kraft is an old client of H&S. Just don't piss him off," Kathy demands.

Hanks laughs. "It's hard not to piss that guy off!"

Jose says, "Well, I think that's it. We all need to communicate with each other throughout the week to make all this happen, and with the holiday coming up, it will just complicate things. Speaking of Christmas, the accounting department is having their annual eggnog party on Friday at 3:00 p.m."

2

AS THE MEETING breaks up, Kathy comes up to me and says, "I'll catch up with you later, so we can talk." I smile.

Jose stops me and says, "Let's meet tomorrow and go through the work plan for the bid. That will give you specific directions about what to do."

"I'd like that," I say.

"As for today, you probably had enough. You can go as you please," Jose says.

"Thanks, Jose." As I walk into my office, I turn off my computer, which never really turned on anyway, pack it in the soft case, and walk down to Hank's office. One knock and "Cone on in," Hanks smiles. "Let's go have a drink to celebrate your first day here. I'll call Denise and see if she wants to come with us."

"Hey, Hank here. Want to join me for a drink after work? We can just go downstairs to Max's."

"Sure, just swing by the cubicle on the way out," Denise says.

Hank and I walk to the accounting department and stop at Denise's cube. She looks at Hank and me and asks, "Who are you?"

"Hi, I'm Loretta, but I'd prefer you call me by my nickname, Lolly."

"Hi, Lolly, I'm Denise. Nice to meet you."

The three of us walk to the elevator lobby and head out of the building and into the alley, heading for Max's Bar and Grill. Max's is an old-fashioned bar with huge semi-circle booths on one side and a huge bar on the other. When we walk in, the bartender points at one of the booths. We sit down, and I realize there is no waitress.

"What can I get for everyone?" Hank asks.

"I'll have a brandy up," Denise says.

"And a Red Zinfandel for me," I say.

Hank returns momentarily with everyone's drinks and sits down. "Cheers, everyone." We all hit our glasses together and take a sip.

"So, Lolly, you're going to work at headquarters for the unforeseen future?" Denise asks.

"Yes. My office is next to Jose's in estimating."

"Lolly was the project manager for the country club project," Hank explains.

"Denise, what do you do at H&S?" I ask.

"I'm a project accountant."

"What projects are you working on?"

"The museum job and One Sansome," Denise states.

"I don't think you were ever the project accountant on my jobs. You would have remembered the parties!" I boast.

We continue to enjoy happy hour and each other's company. I like Denise. She is not high strung. She's simple and pretty—curly hair, medium height, and has a great smile.

"So, tell us about the eggnog party on Friday," Hank says.

"Well, a fellow accountant, Keith, has this killer eggnog recipe that he is very proud of and makes it for us every Christmas," Denise smiles.

"I plan on being there on Friday," I announce.

We have another round and call it a night, even though it's only 6:00 p.m. The parking garage is next to Max's, making it easy. I cross the Golden Gate Bridge, through Marin, and over to East Marin. I walk into the house right as the phone rings. "Hi, this is Loretta."

"Hi, this is Tony. How was your first day back?"

"Hi, I had a good day. How was your day?" I ask.

"I'm ready to relax. Do you want to come over?" Tony asks.

"No, I'm sorry. I'm going to bed and focusing on the rest of the week. I've been assigned to the Coral Towers bid." I explain.

"Hey, we're bidding that job," Tony says.

"What is the estimator's name at Hard Drywall?" I ask.

"Dwayne Tucker," Tony says. "He's the one you will hear from on bid day."

"OK, thanks. I'm just go grab some dinner and hit the sack. It's been a long day. Talk to you tomorrow."

"OK, Lolly. We'll hook up later in the week," Tony says.

"Perfect."

3

I ARRIVE AT headquarters bright and early.

I hope no one expects this of me daily because early is not my thing. The first thing I do is try to find the coffee. I walk down the hall from my office and hear people in a room to the right. I find a small room with a coffee maker, sink, and refrigerator—no table or chairs. The others that were here left after I walked in. Unfortunately, there is no coffee in the pot. They must have finished the pot and left, even though a big sign on the wall says: "It's everyone's job to make coffee. If you took the last cup, someone else isn't going to make it. You are." So, I figured I have to make the next pot even though I didn't drink the last cup. I look around and started opening cabinets, looking for coffee. I look in all the uppers, then all the lowers. No coffee. Maybe we're out. Just as I give up, Jose walks in.

"Good morning, Loretta. You're here early."

"Hi, Jose. Do you know where the coffee is? I ask.

"See the drawer directly below the coffee maker; it's in there, along with the filters," Jose explains.

I turn around, pull the drawer open, and it's full of coffee. "This is brilliant. To put the coffee under the coffee maker—it's too simple, which is why I never looked there. My mom kept her coffee far away from the coffee maker."

"Come to my office after you are done making coffee," Jose says.

Standing and watching coffee brew is like watching grass grow. Finally, I pull two mugs from the cabinet. I found the mugs when I was looking for the coffee. I fill two mugs and walk down the hall into Jose's office.

"It's black. I don't know how you like it," I say.

"Black is perfect," Jose smiles.

It's funny; if Jose had asked me to bring him a cup of coffee, I may have thought that was inappropriate. Now that I went out of my way to bring him a cup, he might think I'm trying to suck up on my second day.

"Come back in five, and we'll start our meeting," Jose says.

"OK."

Five minutes later, I return with my coffee, a tablet, and a pen. I sit at the table in Jose's office, and he joins me.

"I think this will give you a great idea of how we run our bids," Jose describes. "So, we already have purchased a few sets of plans and specs for the Coral Towers project. There is a pre-bid walk on Thursday at 10:00 a.m. You should plan on attending. I will attend, too. At these meetings, which are mandatory to attend if you want to bid on the project, you can figure out your competition, walk the site, and get further instructions.

"Between now and then, the first thing you can do is create a complete scope of work by trade or specification section and then contact subcontractors to confirm if they will be bidding on the job. We have a set of plans and specs in our plan room, next to the elevator lobby, for subs to look at everything we are bidding, do some take-off, and talk to you about the bid. We welcome the subcontractors' input. There is also a sign-in sheet to see who came in."

"I like that," I say.

"It is your responsibility to get to know the project. You don't necessarily need to do take-off *count pieces and parts* on all items, but it helps if you have to come up with a plug number in the bid. Early next week, we'll determine where we are with that. We can also assign bid day responsibilities," Jose sighs. "That was a lot for you to consume. I'll get you a set of plans and specs and a current sub list with names and addresses."

"Thanks, Jose. I think this will keep me plenty busy for the next few days."

After I drive home, I stop at T's to see if she's home. I knock on the door, and Cal answers.

"Lolly, it's so great to see you," Cal says as he rushes to hug me.

"How are you?" I ask.

"I'm fine. Almost done with the Fresno job, here for a little R and R," Cal explains.

"Where's T?" I ask.

"She's inside, opening a bottle of wine. I guess she knew you'd be stopping by," Cal says.

I walk past Cal and into the kitchen. I find T doing exactly that—opening a bottle of wine. I guess she knew I would be stopping by.

"Hey, how are ya?" I ask.

T gives me a big smile. We haven't seen each other for a couple of weeks. She walks over and gives me a big hug. The last time we saw each other was at the yacht club. Since then, "I've been hibernating and haven't gone out for a week. I needed a mental health week. Now, I'm back, working in the estimating department at headquarters in the City," I explain.

"Do you like it?" T asks.

"Well, it's only been two days, but I think it will be OK."

T hands me a glass of wine, and we toast to good friends.

4

I ARRIVE AT headquarters on Wednesday morning, hoping to educate myself on how to bid this job. I started by looking through the plans and reading the specs. Afterward, I call subs to see if they are interested in bidding on the job. I stopped in the plan room to see if any subs signed in for the Coral Towers project. There were four names on the list. I'll make sure I call them later. Then a guy walks in, looks at me, and says, "Hi, I'm Chip with Imperial Acoustics."

"Hi, I'm Loretta. I'm the estimator for the Coral Tower project."

Chip is a tall, tan guy with a dimpled chin and a nice smile.

"Well, I'm here to look at that job. When I'm finished, can I take you to lunch?" Chip asks.

"Uh, I guess so. I've only worked at headquarters for three days, but I'm sure it would be OK," I explain.

"Great," Chip says. "I'll come and find you."

"My office is next to Jose's," I say.

"I'll find you," Chip says.

I walk back to my office and sit down. I look up and see Kathy in the doorway.

"Do you have a minute to talk?" Kathy asks.

"Sure."

"I've been working on the Coral Towers project for a few months. The owner, Centurion Development, is a big client of ours. It will be important if we win this bid," Kathy explains.

I don't want to ruin the relationship with Kathy and the client, but I'm unsure how much control I have over that. It's a competitive bid, and I don't think you get special treatment just because you have a relationship with the client.

"I'll do my best to put in a complete number. Then, don't you have to see where the pricing falls?" I ask.

"Well, of course. However, I have invested a lot in Centurion Development," Kathy explains.

"OK," I say. "I don't know what else to say. There are so many moving parts to putting this bid together; I have no control over the outcome."

I look up, and Chip is standing in the doorway.

"Hi, come on in. This is Kathy, and she was just leaving,"

"Hi, Kathy. I'm Chip with Imperial Acoustics."

"Hi, nice to meet you," she says as she exits my office.

"Are you ready to go to lunch?" Chip asks.

"Yes." I grab my purse and walk out of the office. Chip pokes his head into Jose's office and says, "Hi."

"Hi back," Jose says.

We walk down California Street to Front Street. There are lots of lunch spots around. Chip picks Harrington's, a crowd favorite. We get a table and some menus.

"They have great roast turkey or beef hot gravy sandwiches here," Chip says. "I think they cook a whole turkey every day."

"That's what I'm getting." We order drinks—*I guess that's ok*—and our sandwiches.

"So, how long have you worked for Imperial Acoustics?" I ask.

"I started working straight out of college. My family owns the Company. My Dad will retire in five years and wants me to continue in his shoes," Chip explains.

Chip is a great guy who likes to talk and drink and does a lot of business with H&S. I like him. He's nice to me. After lunch, I told him to call me directly on bid day. I'll make sure his bid gets submitted.

I get back to headquarters, and Jose comes into my office. "So, you went to lunch with Chip?" Jose asks.

"Yes, was that wrong?" I worry.

"Oh, no, we like it when our people establish relationships with the subcontractors," Jose says. "I just wanted to tell you the pre-bid meeting is tomorrow. I'll go with you. It's mandatory to attend if you are going to bid on the job."

"That's fine. What time is it?" I ask.

"9:00 a.m. at the job site. We can meet here at 8:30 a.m. I'll drive," Jose says.

"OK," I say.

I complete my bid list and take another look at the structural drawing before I call it a day. On the way home, the phone rings.

"Hello, this is Loretta."

"Hi, Lolly. It's Tony."

"Hi," I smile.

"Where are you?"

"I'm headed home."

"Me, too. Want to meet me there?" Tony asks.

"Sure, but I can't stay long,"

"Long enough to cook you dinner, I hope."

I smile, "See you soon."

As I pull into the driveway, Tony comes out to meet me. He pulls me out of the car and plants a big kiss on me. I missed him. It's been a few weeks.

"Hi, I missed you."

"I missed you, too,"

Tony smiles, "Come on in and tell me how it is working at headquarters."

I sit down on the couch while Tony delivers two glasses of wine. He sits next to me and kisses me again.

"It's going fine. I'm working on the Coral Towers project. The pre-bid walk is tomorrow morning, so I can't stay out late," I say.

"I'm sure Dwayne will be there," Tony says.

"Good, I get to meet him," I say.

Tony goes to the kitchen to start throwing together the sausage rigatoni for dinner. I set the table and pour us another glass of wine. In no time, Tony serves dinner. He is an amazing cook.

"How is your Mom and Dad?" I ask.

"They ask me about you often," Tony declares. "We'll have to hook up with them at the restaurant someday. How about Friday?"

"Works for me."

5

JOSE AND I leave headquarters at 8:30 a.m. sharp. The job site is south of Market at 2nd and King Street. We park and walk over to the site. I'm glad I wore boots and long pants and not a skirt. Contractors are starting to congregate, and the client waves everyone to the corner to sign in so our attendance is counted. Jose and I move with the pack. Jose moves toward the sign-in sheet. I scan the crowd. Lots of guys say hi to Jose. It's like he knows everyone.

"Welcome, I'm Dave with Centurion Development. This is more or less an opportunity to get a feel for the property, neighborhood, and parking and deliveries to assist with your bid. Bids will be accepted two weeks from today at Centurion's office at 444 Jackson, Suite 201. If you have any questions, submit them to me in writing. I will issue an addendum to the bid documents no later than one week from today."

Jose and I wander back toward where we parked, and a guy comes up to me and asks, "Are you Loretta?"

"Yes, I am, and who are you?"

"I'm Dwayne with Hard Drywall. Tony is a good pal of mine,"

"Wow, Tony said I'd probably meet you during the bid walk. I'm glad Hard Drywall is bidding this job," I say. "Call me directly with your bid. H&S would like to work with Hard Drywall again." Jose introduces himself to Dwayne, and he walks away.

"See, Loretta, you're getting the hang of this already."

Jose and I drive back to headquarters, and it's 11:00 a.m. We walk to the office. Jose asks, "Do you want to grab some lunch with me? There's a great deli just around the corner from the office."

"Sure. That sounds perfect."

"OK. I'll come to get you in a while." Jose says.

I check my messages on my office and my cell number. I have a few. I start answering emails, and Jose walks in and says, "If you are ready, let's go now. I don't feel like standing in line."

"I'm ready."

We walk around the corner to Alli's deli. We were the first ones there, and that made Jose happy. I got a toasted ham and Swiss cheese, and Jose got a turkey and cheddar cheese. Chips for both of us. I order a carton of milk and Jose orders a Diet Coke. We sit, and Jose looks at me and asks, "Do you like estimating so far?"

"Yes, all that has to happen before a bid is amazing. I will try to do everything I must, but this is the first time I took the lead on a bid, so I'm unsure if I will do well."

"I'll make sure you come out of this on top. That doesn't mean we'll win the bid. That means we will submit a complete and thorough bid to Centurion Development and let the process speak for itself." Jose explains.

"OK," I say.

Back at headquarters, Kathy pokes her head in and asks how the pre-bid meeting went.

"Fine," I say.

"That's it. Fine?" Kathy queries.

"Well, Jose knows everybody, so that's good. I'm concentrating on the scope of work. I think we will be well covered by the subs."

"Did you meet Dave from Centurion? Kathy asks.

"No, way too many of us trying to get a word in with Dave," I say. "I think you can focus on Dave, and I'll focus on the subcontractors to bid this job to win."

Kathy looks at me and says, "Sounds good to me."

6

THE FRIDAY BEFORE Christmas is a busy time in the City. There are many company Christmas parties, Friday shoppers, and visiting tourists. However, at H&S, we already had our company Christmas party two weeks ago, and today is the special eggnog celebration at 3:00 p.m. We congregate in the accounting department and anticipate the current batch of Keith's family's eggnog recipe. I wander toward the accounting department and spot Hank and Denise. They have eggnog in hand. I approach them and ask, "How are you guys?"

"Hi, Lolly. We're glad you made it to our eggnog shindig," Denise says.

"I wouldn't miss it for the world," I say. "I don't even know if I like eggnog," I proclaim.

"You will like this eggnog. I'll get you a glass."

Denise maneuvers through the crowd to get to Keith's bucket of eggnog.

"I need another glass for a new gal in estimating."

"Well, where is she? I would like to meet her," Keith says.

Denise throws up an arm, indicating a request for me to come over and meet Keith. I make my way to the eggnog bucket.

"Hi, I'm Lolly."

"Hi, I'm Keith."

"Thanks for making the eggnog," I say.

"It's a holiday tradition for the accounting department."

I smile, and he hands me a glass. I make my way back to Denise and Hank.

"I don't think I've ever tasted something so good," I say. "I didn't even think I liked eggnog."

"How can you not like this?" Hank asks. "Just be careful because it's very strong."

"Like alcohol-wise?" I ask.

"Yes, the recipe has been passed down in my family, and we don't share it with many friends," Keith shares. "It's too dangerous."

"OK," I say.

"Any plans for the weekend?" I ask Denise and Hank.

"I'm finishing shopping for my family," Denise says.

"I'm going to the 49er's game on Sunday," Hank says excitingly.

"Wow. Great. I'm going to head out. Have fun."

I head to Larkspur to Tony's restaurant, Bertelli's. I call Tony to tell him I'm on the way.

"Hi, this is Tony."

"Hi, this is Lolly."

"Hi, where are you? I'm almost to the restaurant."

"I just left the City. I'm probably twenty minutes out."

"OK. I'll be here waiting for you," Tony says.

I think about his mom and dad and how good it will be to see them. I pull into the parking lot and walk to the front door. Tony meets me with a big hug and kiss.

"Hi, sweetie."

"Hi, Tony."

We walk into the restaurant to his favorite table. His mom and dad are already seated there.

"Hi, Loretta," his mom says.

"Hi, Maria. Hi, Vinnie," I say with a smile. Tony hugs his mom and dad and leads me to a seat. I sit and smile. Tony sits next to me and puts his arm around me.

"Tell Lolly about Uncle Luca's trip to visit us," Vinnie says.

"Uncle Luca lives in Tuscany, Italy. He has a forty-acre vineyard and a rustic winery. He came to visit my dad years ago when the sausage company was just getting started. My grandpa wanted him to stay, but he couldn't leave Tuscany. Now, he is visiting us for two weeks after all these years. He wants to go to the wine country and taste California wines. He wants to see the restaurant and deli business for himself," Tony tells me.

"That sounds great. When is he coming?" I ask.

"I think it's in May," Maria says. "He hasn't confirmed his plans, but he will soon."

"I like the Christmas decorations in the restaurant, by the way."

"They are so old," Maria reveals.

"Maybe that's why I like them," I admit.

Angelo serves all our favorites, along with one of Uncle Luca's wines. It's Cabernet Sauvignon by CalaLuca, the name of Uncle Luca's Winery. He told us it was the two places together when he named it.

"Everything was fabulous, including the wine," I say.

"I'm really looking forward to Uncle Luca's visit," Tony says. "He's doing very well in Tuscany, and I want to hear all about it."

Tony looks at me and says, "Are you ready to go?"

"Yes. I had a lovely time. Bye, Maria and Vinnie. It was great to see you again," I say.

Tony pulls out my chair and helps me stand. We approach Maria and Vinnie, exchange hugs, and exit the restaurant. Tony asks, "Are you following me?"

"Yes, I am."

7

THE NEXT WEEK was very busy. I talked to 200 subcontractors to confirm they are bidding on Coral Tower, helped Jose with leveling sheets for bid day, and helped set up the bid day computer spreadsheet. We are all set for next week. I walk down to the accounting department and find Denise. She was walking up to me as I was approaching her cube.

"Hi, Denise. How are you?" I ask.

"Fine."

"Want to go out for a drink later?" I ask.

"Sure," Denise says.

"I'll swing by at 5:00 p.m., and we can just go downstairs," I say.

"There's another little bar a block away that we can try if you want," Denise says.

"That's fine. I'll see you in a little while," I smile and walk back down the hall. I return to my office, and Kathy follows me in and sits down before I do. I sit, look at her, and ask, "What can I do for you?"

"I'm glad you asked because I need your help," Kathy explains. "I need you to fill out a questionnaire about H&S."

"Do you think I'm the most competent to fill this out?"

"No, but no one has time for me, and I figured I'd try you," Kathy explains.

"You'd try me. This doesn't sound right. Doesn't anyone in the company help you with stuff like this?" I ask.

"I struggle to get anyone to participate," Kathy admits.

"Don't they understand that you are trying to get work for the company and keep them all employed?"

"I think they do, but I don't think they think they have to do anything to get new work—like it's not their job. But it's everyone's job to get new work," Kathy states.

My phone rings, and Kathy leaves my office. I pick up the phone, "Hi, this is Loretta."

"Hi, this is Tony."

"Hi, I'm still at work and going out for a drink with an accountant named Denise. You'd love her."

"OK, I'll talk to you tomorrow," Tony says.

I pack my computer and walk down to Denise's cube. She sees me approaching and stands up.

"I'm ready," Denise says.

"Me, too." I smile as we walk toward the elevator, through the lobby, and onto the sidewalk. I look at Denise and ask, "Now where?"

Denise points, "Down Kearny Street and then down Pine Street to an alley."

"What's the name of the place?" I ask.

"Bud's," Denise smiles.

We walk in. There is hardly any room for us at the bar, but we find two spots. The bartender comes over immediately and asks, "What can I get you?"

"I'll have a brandy up," Denise says.

"And I'll have a glass of Red Zinfandel," I say. As the bartender leaves, I ask, "So, where do you live?"

Denise says, "In the Mission District."

"Do you take the bus or drive to work? I'm unfamiliar with public transit other than BART, and once you get to the City, BART is limited."

"The bus works great within a block of my flat. Where do you live?" Denise asks.

"I live in East Marin, across the Bay."

"Sounds nice."

"It's near the water, which is like open space," I respond. "Who do you work for?" I ask.

"I work for Josh Ryan, the accounting manager. Have you met him?" Denise asks.

"No."

"He gets in at 8:00 a.m., goes to lunch at noon, and leaves at 5:00 p.m. I could tell time by his routine," Denise says. "He's sort of a nerdy guy, shorter, glasses—an accountant."

"So, do you know Kathy Sullivan? She came to talk to me today to ask for help," I explain.

"I know her. She comes out for drinks with Hank and me occasionally. I don't think the operation guys give her the time of day, except Hank and Dan, because that's their job."

"Did you go to a meeting with all of them?"

"Yes, on Monday."

We order two more drinks.

8

IT'S FINALLY BID day. Jose organizes the bid room bins by specification section. Three project managers are helping with the bid today. The bid is at 2:00 p.m. Jose told everyone to get to the bid room by 11:00 a.m. Lunch will be served.

I get to work early to make sure the scope of work is covered, and I have a good handle on the trades with the biggest impact on the bid. I created the leveling sheets. I like to call them apples and oranges sheets because they are used to make all the bids apples and keep the oranges separate. You have to be ready when the bids start coming in. Kathy will be delivering the bid form to Centurion Development and will make sure the bid form is properly signed by Harry Henderson well before 2:00 p.m.

This morning, Jose and I fill in the bid summary spreadsheet with plug numbers, or guesstimates, to get to the bottom line of the cost of the work. Hank and Dan are working on H&S's cost to manage the work and any other general requirement costs to include in the bid.

The first pass, we're at $31 million. Soft costs are at $1.86 million. As the bids come in, they are analyzed and leveled, and the low sub-number will be input into the spreadsheet and replace the plug number. It all must happen quickly and accurately.

By 11:15, all of us had lunch, and some bids were coming in and being placed in the appropriate bins. We won't start analyzing the bids until noon. I sit at the computer. Jose walks up and down the bin board, looking at bids. Each bin has a plug in the computer, so Jose knows what it is.

"Loretta, why don't you come up here with me and let Mark work on the computer? You know the scope of work better than anyone. Start reviewing these with me," Jose says.

I switch places with Mark and start to read the bids. I talk out loud.

"Landscaping—Valley landscaping is low. Structural steel—Herrick plus architectural steel, so Herrick is not high bidder. We need to add $120,000 to other steel bids."

"Good call, Loretta," Jose smiles.

"Drywall—Hard Drywall. Painting—Colorama. Elevator—Otis. We still need fire sprinklers and paving and grading. Steve is leveling the HVAC. Mark has plumbing, and Chris has electrical.

"Mark, can you do both your leveling sheet for plumbing and the computer?" I ask.

"The plumbing scope is pretty straightforward, and I already have four bids and an apparent low bidder," Mark states.

"Good. Put it in the bin and concentrate on input from Jose and me for now," I instruct.

"OK," Mark says.

I look at Jose and say, "Everything alright?"

"Yes."

"I'm taking a bathroom break before it gets crazy." Jose says, "Go."

I was only gone a few minutes, and the activity already picked up. I move back to the bins and pick up two more bids. "Looks like Hard is still low. I move to acoustical and

Imperial Acoustics appears low, although there is only one other bid."

"1:30 p.m.," Jose screams. "Everyone finalize what you are doing."

Hank and Dan walk in and sit with Jose and me at the table. I look at their numbers for general requirements. "I don't see a number for temporary offices inside while we move the trailers and complete paving."

"Another good call," Jose says.

"With that added, the total management cost is $1.799 million. You like that number?" Hank asks.

"Right now, we are at $30.7 million. Electrical and HVAC are still out." Jose starts looking over Mark's shoulder as I keep looking for new bids.

"Where do we still have plugs? Jose asks.

"Rebar and fire sprinklers," Mark says.

"Loretta, call these subs and see if you can get bids," Jose screams. I run to my office and rush to see what I can come up with. Five minutes later, I return with a bid for each. Our plugs were not that far off.

"Get the numbers from Steve and Chris," Jose yells.

They run into the bid room. It's 1:50 p.m. The numbers are input, and we are at $30.55 million. Kathy calls and is on hold for the final number. Just then, Harry walks into the room and asks, "Jose, where are we at?"

"We're at $30.55 million."

"Cut $350,000," Harry instructs. Jose does the math. "Get Kathy on the phone… Kathy, are you ready? The number is $30.2 million." Jose says anxiously. "Thirty million, two hundred thousand. Go!"

I hang the phone up, and I'm breathing heavily. I look at Jose and ask, "Is it like this every time?"

Harry and the others who helped with the bid were already gone. Jose looks at me. "Sit down. Relax. It's over.

Bids are usually hectic. This one went fine, thanks to you," Jose acknowledges.

"Where will we come up with a $350,000 cut right at bidtime?" I ask.

"Lots of money can move around after a bid. You find some and need some more, but it's funny because you usually come out even. Sometimes, we find bid busts and double something up on others. However, that's rare with good estimators. You're a good estimator, Loretta. Thanks for all your hard work."

I smile at Jose, and just then, the phone rings. It's Kathy.

"Hi, Kathy," Jose says, almost stuttering. "Let me write this down." Jose is writing while I try to listen.

"OK. Thanks, Kathy. See you tomorrow," Jose says.

"Well?"

"We didn't get the job."

9

I WANDER BACK to my office after my offer to help Jose straighten up the bid room is refused. I sit at my desk and stare out the window into the alley. I feel like something is missing. If we didn't get the project, we don't have subcontracts to hire, ground-breaking ceremonies to attend, new clients, architects, and engineers to meet, new staff to team up, and a job site to move into. I had my heart set on running this job. I'm feeling lost.

I pull into T's house on the way home. She'll cheer me up. T opens the door even before I knock.

"Come on in. I'm glad you're here," T says.

"I'm glad I'm here, too," I say.

"What's wrong?" T asks.

"Well, I've been working on a bid for the last two weeks. It bid today. H&S didn't get the job," I respond.

"Not because of anything you did, right?" T asks.

"Oh, God, no. There are lots of us working together to pull a bid off," I explain. "It's just that H&S needs the work, and I need a job to go to," I say as T hands me a glass of wine.

"Thanks. What's new with you?" I ask.

"Well, Cal is visiting his family in San Diego, so I've been hanging here myself. I sort of like it because I can organize some things when he's not here. It's just easier," T says.

"You two still good?" I ask.

"Absolutely. His mom had hip surgery, and he decided to hang out with her," T explains.

"Is he like the best guy, or what?" I smile.

"How's Tony?"

"We ate at the restaurant last week. I saw his mom and dad and spent the night at his place, but I haven't seen him since. But we're all good, too," I smile.

The next day, I show up at headquarters, grab a cup of coffee, and carry it to Jose's office. "Good morning, Loretta," Jose smiles. "Sit down."

"Thanks. I'm curious about what's next." I say.

"Well, go talk to Kathy about Goldman Sachs. It's a tenant improvement in One Sansome, top three floors."

"I am a little disappointed that we didn't get the job," I admit.

"Everyone is, but the lowest bid was $29.1 million. We could never do it for that."

"Thanks for talking. I'll talk to Kathy and see what she needs me to do."

I go to get another cup of coffee and settle in my office. The next thing I know, Kathy is in my office, sitting in front of me.

"Good morning," I say. "What can I do for you?"

"Hank told me you were going to be working on the Goldman Sachs proposal, and I should come talk to you," Kathy says.

"I know nothing. I need plans and specs. I'd like to visit the site and meet the owner's rep."

"What are you doing for lunch today? I can see if Bob Kraft can join us for lunch."

"That's fine. Let me know."

The next thing I know, Kathy and I are in Harrington's, waiting for Bob to arrive. Bob walks in and sees us at the table across the room. Kathy stands to greet him as he approaches the table.

"Hi Bob, I'd like to introduce you to Loretta Novak. She will be the project manager on this project if we sign a contract with you."

"Nice to meet you, Bob. I'm Loretta."

"Are you currently on another project?" Bob asks.

"No, I'm in the office estimating."

"What was the last project you were on?"

"The Golden Gate Country Club project."

The waiter approaches and hands us menus.

"I'll have the hot turkey sandwich and a black coffee," I say.

"I'll have the same," Bob says.

"Make it three, with an iced tea."

"Thanks," the waiter says. "I'll be right back with your drinks. Sir, did you want a drink?"

"Water is fine, thanks," Bob says.

"So, Bob, tell us a little about the Goldman Sachs project," Kathy says.

"Well, Goldman Sachs is moving into the top three floors of One Sansome. It is roughly 54,000 square feet and will house their Bay Area executives and the main trading room. They are relocating from Montgomery Street. They have a construction team from New York managing the project," Bob explains.

"How are they selecting a contractor?" I ask.

"I'm holding contractor interviews when their team is here, which should be sometime next week."

With that, our lunch was served. I thought it was interesting Goldman Sachs had a team from New York to manage the job. Bob is obviously on our side. We finish our lunch. I pay. I ask if scheduling a walk through the site would be OK.

"Just call my office. We will arrange something," Bob says before leaving the restaurant.

Kathy and I walk back up California Street and return to headquarters.

When we arrive, I say, "What I really need is a set of plans and specs."

"I'll make sure you get one. Thanks for lunch. I'll keep you posted on the interview," Kathy says.

10

I WANDER BACK to my office after lunch to fill out an expense report for lunch. I find the form, which is double-sided. You have to attach the receipts to a blank page with scotch tape and note who was at the lunch and the reason for it. I attached my receipt and wrote, "Kathy Sullivan and Bob Kreft from Goldman Sachs."

I forgot to include the parking tag, so I need to fill out another expense report for the parking tag. I get another piece of paper. I stick a piece of tape on my receipt for the parking tag, write "Loretta Novak–monthly parking," and attach it to the expense report. The next thing I do is gather an interoffice envelope, put in the two expense reports, scratch the names on the envelopes, write "HANK EVANS" in the blank spaces on the envelope, and put them in the outbox. Each office has an in box and an out box.

The plans and specs for Goldman Sachs arrived, and I started to get familiar with the plans. Hank, Kathy, and I will meet later in the week to discuss strategy for Goldman Sachs. The interview is scheduled for next Wednesday at 2:00 p.m. at Bob Kreft's office. The superintendent, Eddie Kramer, and I will attend with Hank. They are not asking for pricing, just a completed request for proposal. Usually, when the client doesn't ask for an estimate, it means the architect is behind on their design or the client has trouble making decisions. Either way, the project's schedule is what suffers.

My expense checks were delivered via interoffice mail today. I immediately remove them from the envelope, tear them apart, turn them over, and sign the backs. I'll go to the bank and deposit them after lunch. I grab a soup around the corner and then slip into the bank to deposit my checks. I feel like it's Friday. I'm ready for some different scenery. The yacht club for happy hour sounds perfect. When I get back to the office, I call Tony.

"Hi, this is Tony."

"Hi, this is Lolly."

"Well, hi, I was just thinking about you," Tony says.

"Want to go to the yacht club for happy hour, say around 5:30?" I ask.

"I can't. I said I'd help at the restaurant tonight. Go pick up T and Cal. They'd love that view."

"Cal is in San Diego with his mom, so T and I can go. Think we can do something this weekend?"

Tony smiles, "Yes, I'll call Saturday. Have fun with T at the club."

I stop by T's to see if she's up for the yacht club. It is usually very busy on Fridays. T opens the door in her house clothes. She must be working around the house.

"Hi, whatcha doing?" I ask.

"Spring cleaning. I told you I'd probably use the time that Cal was gone to do a little organizing," T explains.

I might just sit on my deck tonight and look at the view. That would be the perfect distraction.

I join Jose for a cup of coffee on Monday morning to get up to speed on the week's buzz. On my way back to my office after a coffee refill, I am followed by Josh Ryan, the

San Francisco accounting manager, and Patty Shone, CFO of H&S.

"Do you have a minute for us to talk to you?" Patty asks.

"Sure. Come on in," I say.

They walk into my office and shut the door behind them. I sit at my desk, and Ryan and Patty sit forward on the chairs with curious eyes.

"So, what can I do for you?" I ask.

"We have a few questions for you," Patty says. She pulls out one of my expense checks and asks, "Is this your expense check?"

"Yes," I reply.

She turns the check over and asks, "Is this your signature?"

"Yes."

She pulls another check out and asks, "Is this your signature?"

"Yes, it is," I say.

Patty turns the second check over and asks, "Is this your name? The name on the check is Lynsey Miller."

"No, it's not my name," I say, flustered.

"So, why is your signature on the back of that check?" Patty asks.

"I'm puzzled that this is happening. I was expecting two checks. I received two checks. The checks were attached to each other. I removed them from the interoffice mail. I tore them apart. I turned them over, signed both of them, and took them to the bank. I guess I didn't think anything else of it."

"I guess, in the future, you should pay a little more attention to the name on your check you sign. Someone may have made an error. We will have to have a conversation with our bank, too. They should have never cashed the check that you signed."

"So, I'm not going to jail?" I ask.

"No, we'll let you off this time," Patty smiles.

11

I AM VERY familiar with the Goldman Sachs plans and specs and feel confident about our interview tomorrow. However, I'm getting cold and sweaty, like I'm coming down with something.

The next morning, I can hardly get out of bed to call in sick. This doesn't happen often—*I'm a pretty healthy individual*—but there is no way I can make it to the office today. Hacking, flehm, watery eyes, runny nose, the works. I call Hank. He answers the phone, "Hi, this is Hank."

"Hi, this is Lolly," I say with a scratchy, dry voice.

"Hi, Lolly. Are you OK? You sound horrible," Hank says.

"No, I've got a nasty flu, and being far from a bathroom is not a good idea, so I need to stay home today."

"OK, feel better. We'll fill you in on how the interview goes."

"Thanks, Hank," I respond as I blow my nose in Kleenex.

Hanks calls Kathy. "Hi, this is Kathy."

"Hi, this is Hank. Loretta is sick and will not be at the interview today. She sounds horrible."

"Do you or Eddie know anything about the job?" Kathy asks. "I know Loretta spent a lot of time learning about this job. What about the schedule? Does Eddie know anything about the schedule?"

"I don't know what he knows," Hank says.

"Well, I think Loretta is going to have to come in and go to the interview," Kathy explains. "We are not going to have a chance without her."

"I'll call her and see if that is even possible," Hank states. He hangs up and calls Lolly.

"Hi, this is Loretta," I say, half asleep.

"Hi, this is Hank. How are you feeling?"

Silence.

"I'm calling because Kathy thinks we don't have a chance in hell at this job if you are not at the interview. I know this isn't right, but we need you to come to work for this interview. Are you there?"

"I'm here," cough, cough. "Do I have a choice?"

"No, not really," Hank says. "It will only take no more than an hour, plus the commute. You'd need to leave like now to get here in time."

"Can I wear my pajamas?" I ask.

"Just get here by 1:00 p.m. The interview is at 2:00 p.m. We will owe you one after this," Hank says.

I drag myself into the bathroom, afraid to look in the mirror. I must be ready in ten minutes. This is not what I want to be doing, but I head into the office. By the time I get there, it's 1:00 p.m. I sit down, almost sweating to death. I take a few deep breaths and close my eyes.

"Hi, Loretta," Kathy says. "You don't look too good."

"No shit. I'm sick. I'm here, though," I share.

"We can just walk to the interview, but will you be able to keep up?" Hank asks as he walks into my office.

"Can we get a cab? I know it's only a few blocks, but that would be a problem for me."

Somehow, Hank, Eddie, and I make it to One Sansome early. We make our way to the twelfth floor for our interview. The three of us sit down in a conference room. Bob Kraft walks in. Hank introduces Eddie and me to Bob. Just then, two more gentlemen walk into the conference room. Bob stands up.

"Let me introduce you to the Goldman Sachs construction management team from New York. This is David and Simon from Goldman Sachs, who will manage the project. David and Simon, this is Loretta, Eddie, and Hank from H&S."

"Can you introduce yourselves and explain your role on the project?" Simon asks.

"Certainly, Hank says. "I am Hank. I am the operations manager for the interiors group and will oversee the project. We have been the general contractor for five other tenants in this building, so we are familiar with the rules and regulations. We've worked with Bob, and we have worked with the architect, before, as well."

"Thanks, Hank Evans. We would like to hear from Loretta," Bob says.

"Hi, I'm Loretta Novak, the proposed project manager for this project. It's nice to meet you, Simon and David. My main concern on this project is the delivery of the Sonoshades for the balconies. If you have a fourteen-week construction schedule, you would have to order them on day one, and they are a sole source, which means you can't shop around for a better delivery date," I say.

"Eddie, would you like to add anything to the conversation?" David asks.

"I'm Eddie Cramer, the superintendent on the job. Working in downtown San Francisco is unique, and I have experience in this building and many others." Eddie says.

We all stand up. "Thanks for meeting with us today," Simon says. "We will decide on a general contractor in a week or so. We wanted to let you know that you won't get any bonus points for bringing her because the other general contractor also brought a female."

Just as I start to lunge forward, Eddie and Hank grab my arms, one on each side, and hold me back from what I really want to say, but I am too sick to say it. My head is pounding. I feel like crap, and hearing that makes me want to… I collapse right into the guys' arms. They put me back onto the chair. No one knows what to do. When I came to, I was shivering cold. I have a fever and want to leave.

Hank and Eddie try again. They stand me up and help walk me out of the conference room. Hank turns back and says, "Sorry about that. Loretta was sick today, but we thought it would be a good idea if she still came along to the interview. Maybe not."

12

I STAY HOME the day after the interview. I still feel like crap and feel even worse about fainting in the conference room at the interview. I lay low for the rest of the week and finally got a chance to call Tony.

"Hi, this is Tony."

"Hi, this is Lolly."

"Hi. I'm so glad you called. I miss you. And guess what?"

"What?"

"Uncle Luca is here on his two-week vacation. I need to plan a few days of wine tasting. But first, you are invited to a family dinner at the restaurant on Friday at 5:00 p.m. Can you join us?" Tony asks.

"I would like that. I'll come straight from work if that's OK," I say.

"Sure, that would be fine," Tony says. "I'm so excited for you to meet Uncle Luca."

Friday seems to drag along, especially since I am looking forward to dinner tonight. I head out of the City at 4:30 p.m., over the Golden Gate Bridge, and into Larkspur. As soon as I pull into Bertelli's parking lot, Tony runs out and greets me. He opens the Miata door, grabs my hand, lifts me out, and wraps me in his arms. I hug him back. Then, I move away and look at him. He does the same and smiles. He pulls my hand and says, "Let's go. Uncle Luca's waiting."

Once inside, we walk to Uncle Luca's table. "No, don't stand up. Uncle Luca, this is my girlfriend, Loretta, but we call her Lolly." Luca reaches over to my hand. "It's a pleasure to finally meet you. Tony always talks about you."

"The pleasure is all mine, Uncle Luca. We want to hear some stories about Tuscany," I say.

"Come and sit with me at my table. We can start with our first bottle of Calaluca before dinner," Luca says.

"We need to say hi to a few more people, and we'll be right back," Tony says. He grabs my hand, and we walk over to Maria and Vinnie.

"Lolly, you made it," Maria says.

"I wouldn't miss this dinner—ever," I say. "Hi, Vinnie."

"You look beautiful tonight, Lolly," Vinnie says.

"Why, thank you," I smile.

Tony pulls me back to Uncle Luca's table as if we are missing out on something if we don't hurry back. *Oh, the wine.* Luca has already uncorked the Calaluca Primativo and poured three glasses.

We each take a glass. Luca holds his glass up and says, "Here's to Tony and Lolly." We all cheers and take a sip.

"So, tell us about Tuscany. What's the weather like? What kind of grapes do you grow?" Tony asks.

"Well, the weather in Tuscany is very similar to northern California. Hot and dry in the summer, milder and rainier in spring and autumn, and the winter is wetter and colder, especially at night. So, with a similar climate, some familiar names exist in Tuscany—Sangiovese, Cabernet, Syrah, and Merlot. While I'm here, I would like to find some wineries with Sangiovese and Syrah, maybe some Primativo. Can you and Tony help me with that?" Luca asks.

Angelo serves some calamari and bruschetta. Perfect.

"I would love to go wine tasting with you and Tony this weekend," I respond with a smile.

"We can do a little research to find the varietals Luca is looking for," Tony says.

We all start in on our appetizers. The CalaLuca wine is great. Maybe they should sell that brand at the deli. Dinner is served as well. The lasagna is fabulous. Uncle Luca is enjoying his meal. Everyone is.

"So, what time should we meet to head up to Healdsburg?" Tony asks.

Luca says, "How about 11:00 a.m.? That way, I can spend the morning acclimating to the time zone."

"We'll plan on dinner here tomorrow, as well," Tony says.

With that, Tony and I stand, say goodnight to Uncle Luca and Tony's parents and leave the restaurant. As we get to my car, Tony kisses me. I pull away and say, "I'm going home tonight. You can come along."

"No, just plan on staying at my house tomorrow," Tony says.

"That will work. I'll see you at 11:00 a.m. tomorrow," I respond and kiss him goodnight.

13

THE NEXT DAY, I woke up thinking of our Uncle Luca wine tour. We can start in Geyserville. Trentadue Winery has a nice Sangiovese. The next stop can be Davero Farms and Winery on Westside Road. Then, we can head into Healdsburg and hit Ramey Winery and Quivera Winery for their Syrah.

I drive back to Bertelli's to meet Tony and Uncle Luca. Tony invites me in for a latte, and I share my plan with them. They like it.

Our first stop is Trentadue Winery in Geyserville. The grounds are beautiful, and they host a lot of weddings here. We head to the tasting room. Uncle Luca is wandering around the space while Tony and I go to the bar.

"Good morning. Three for tasting," Tony says, even though it is still morning.

A gal named Lisa provided the day's tasting list and three glasses. "Would you like to start with whites?" Lisa asks.

"No, we'll go straight to reds. We are particularly interested in Sangiovese. My uncle lives in Tuscany and has a winery there. We are here exploring northern California Sangiovese, and this is our first stop," Tony explains.

Uncle Luca comes to the tasting bar after exploring the whole place.

"Did you take notes?" Tony asks.

"This is wonderful. It's exactly what I wanted to see and learn," Luca says.

"How about tasting some wine?" Lisa asks.

"Absolutely," Luca says.

"Here is a list of what we are pouring today," Lisa explains.

"How about we start with the Sangiovese since that's why we came here," I say.

"Great," Lisa says. She reaches for the bottle and pours short sips of the wine for each of us. "This wine is made entirely from the Block 602 Brunello Clone. The weather and the precise timing of irrigation—or lack of it—decreases the berry size of the Sangiovese significantly, contributing to more concentration and intensity in the wine. In addition to the Asian spices, dried cranberries, and bright cherries, there are deeper and more complex aromas and flavors of dark stone fruit and blackberries. The oak aging adds additional aromas of vanilla, maple, toast, and a hint of cinnamon to the already spicy and complex wine."

"Uncle Luca, what do you think?" Tony asks.

Luca picks up the glass, swirls the wine, sniffs it, and takes a sip. Tony and I do the same.

"This is a complex, spicy wine. I love it," Luca says.

"Do you want to taste anything else?" Lisa asks.

"No, but I would like to buy a bottle," Luca says.

Lisa prepares the sale, and we thank her for the service and move on to the next winery.

We go to Davero Farms and Winery on Westside Road in Sonoma County. We enter the winery. The bar is rustic. Maybe that's like Luca's winery.

Again, Luca wanders around, taking in everything, from the finishes to the layout. Tony and I make our way to the tasting bar and request three glasses for tasting. Bob returns with the glasses and the tasting menu. By the time Luca returns to the tasting bar, Bob, who has a name tag on, has us set up for a Barbera pour.

Luca tells Bob he's more interested in a taste of Sangiovese, and Bob returns with two varieties. He pours tastes for the three of us, and Luca grabs his glass. Luca picks up the glass, swirls the wine, sniffs it, and takes a sip. Tony and I do the same, again.

Luca likes the Dry Creek Sangiovese the best, and we buy a bottle and leave. We head to Ramey Winery in Healdsburg. We walk through a ten-foot door to a fabulous tasting room. A guy approaches. "Hi, welcome to Ramey Winery. My name is David, and I am the owner of Ramey." Luca is looking at the barrel room to the left of the tasting bar, and Tony and I stand across from David.

"It's nice to meet you. My uncle is here from Tuscany to explore Sonoma County wines. Three for tasting," Tony requests.

David waits for Luca to return to the tasting bar, holds his hand out, and says, "I'm David, the owner and winemaker here."

"What a pleasure to meet you. I'm Luca. I'm here to learn more about wines in Sonoma," Luca says.

"Well, you came to the right place. I will be serving you today. Do you have a particular wine you would like to taste?" David asks.

"Syrah," Luca replies.

"Perfect. We have three Syrahs for tasting. We can start with our Sonoma County Syrah, made from grapes grown right here at the winery property. It's very inky and has strong flavors of licorice and pepper." He pours us all a taste. Luca picks up the glass, swirls the wine, sniffs it, and takes a sip. Tony and I do the same, again.

"Well, Luca, what do you think?" David asks.

Luca smiles and says, "I'm glad we came here. This wine has a familiar taste to me. I like that in a wine."

"Thank you, Luca. I've been making wine all my life, and it makes me happy hearing that from you," David explains.

"I've been making wine all my life, too," Luca says.

"Ready for the next taste?" David asks.

Tony and I look at each other, and I say, "We are."

"The next Syrah is grown in the Dry Creek Valley, a few miles from here, but with a similar climate. It has a full nose and a great finish," David says as he pours the taste.

Luca picks up the glass, swirls the wine, sniffs it, and takes a sip. Tony and I do the same, again.

Luca says, "This wine is fantastic. I can still smell and taste it."

"That's that great finish," David smiles. "Let's get you our last Syrah, which is 89 percent Syrah and 11 percent Zinfandel. I don't know if you like blends, Luca, but this one calms the Syrah down and enhances the flavor. This is my personal favorite," he continues as he pours our last tastes.

Luca picks up the glass, swirls the wine, sniffs it, and takes a sip. Tony and I do the same, again.

"I see what you mean, David. This has a flavor all its own," Luca says. "Well, I would like to buy a bottle of each of the Syrahs. If you ever come to Tuscany, David, be sure to visit CalaLuca Winery, and I will be able to return the favor. Are you two ready to go?

"Yes, we're ready. Thanks, David. We all enjoyed it," Tony says.

"Thanks, David. It couldn't have been any better," I add.

We all walk out of there with smiles on our faces, maybe because of the wine and maybe because of David.

"We don't have to go anywhere else. I'm done," Luca says.

"That's fine," Tony says. "Let's just head back to the restaurant and get some dinner. It's been a long, productive day.

14

WE GET BACK to Bertelli's. Luca is still smiling. We get all his purchases out of the car and carry them into the restaurant. We sit at Tony's favorite table, and Angelo immediately appears.

"Where have you all been?" Angelo asks.

"We took Uncle Luca to explore Sonoma County wineries today. We're ready for some food," Tony says.

"Do you want a bottle of wine?" Angelo asks.

Luca hands him a bottle of Sangiovese that he bought at Trentadue. "This will work. Can we start with the regular starters, please?" Luca smiles.

Angelo takes the bottle and rushes off to get us some food. Luca looks around, smiles, and says, "Thanks for taking me today."

Angelo rushes back with an uncorked bottle of Sangiovese and pours three glasses.

"You're welcome, Uncle Luca. We both had a great time with you today," Tony says. "I'm glad you enjoyed it."

"Tony, I would like to ask you something. Today made it seem possible that something could happen—something I've been thinking about," Luca says.

"Uncle Luca, what are you talking about?" Tony asks.

"I'd like you to come to Tuscany and work with me. I could teach you the wine business, how to grow grapes, and how to sell wine, but you would be in Italy. Lolly would be here. It would only be for six months, but I think that's all it would take to learn what you need to have your own winery in Sonoma County when you return. What do you say?" Luca asks.

For a moment, Tony and my jaws drop. We are shocked, listening to what Luca is saying, but it doesn't sink in. "Tony would be gone for six months" is all I heard.

"Uncle Luca, thank you very much for the offer to teach me the art of wine. Right now, I'm overwhelmed by this. I need some time to think about it and talk to Lolly," Tony explains.

The food arrives at the table, and today, it's lasagna. Everyone gets quiet and starts eating. The Sangiovese—*I love just saying the word, Sangio-vese*—is spectacular.

Tony's parents walk in.

"Well, look at this crew," Vinnie laughs.

"Sit down. Join us. We'll tell you all about our day," Uncle Luca says.

As Maria and Vinnie sit, Angelo grabs two more glasses and pours the wine.

"Don't worry, there is more where that came from," Luca states. "So, Lolly and Tony took me wine tasting today. You are tasting the Sangiovese I bought at Trentadue. Next, we stopped at Davero, but my favorite was Ramey, where we met the owner and winemaker. I invited him to Tuscany to visit my winery. I also invited Tony to work with me at CalaLucas for six months."

It gets very quiet again. Vinnie looks at Tony, and Maria looks at me. Then, Maria and Vinnie look at Uncle Luca and say, "What?!" Tony and I don't say a word.

"Calm down. Tony hasn't accepted my offer yet. I just asked him thirty minutes ago. It's only for six months.

"Where would he live?" Maria asks. "Who would pay for his travel?"

"Let's let him decide if he even wants to do it; then, we can work on the details," Luca says, talking as if Tony wasn't sitting at the table with them. "I'm here for two more days. He needs to decide by then."

Tony stands, looks at me, and asks, "Are you ready to go?" He looks back at everyone at the table. "Lolly and I have to talk about this. I'll check in tomorrow. Good night."

I stand, wave, grab Tony's hand, and walk out the door, still in shock.

We both drive to Tony's. Once inside his house, the first thing we do is open a bottle of wine. It could be a long night. We sit at the dining room table, and Tony pours the wine.

I take a sip. "So, talk to me. What are you thinking?" I ask.

"Wow. That came out of the blue. I was not expecting that from Uncle Luca, nor were my parents. I would have thought he would have talked to them before throwing it out to me," Tony shares. "What do you think of it all?"

"Is it something you want to learn to do?" I ask. I mean, to grow grapes, make wine, sell wine, and run a winery?"

Tony takes a sip. "I would love to learn the wine business, but I could probably do that here and not be away from you for six months."

I take a sip. "All I heard Luca say initially was 'six months,' but Tony, this might be an opportunity of a lifetime—to live in Italy and learn from a pro, and it's *only* six months."

"Won't you miss me?" Tony asks as he takes another sip.

"Of course, I will miss you, silly, but you can send lots of pictures of CalaLuca Winery and Tuscany," I smile.

"Where would I live? What would I do with this place and my truck?"

"It sounds like you are warming up to the idea. Why don't we sit here and make a list of questions to ask Uncle Luca," I say.

Once Tony is over the shock of the whole thing, he starts to see how great of an offer this is. We call it a night and vow to make the list tomorrow.

15

TONY AND I had a great evening. Our minds were racing, and we didn't get much sleep, thinking about the possibility of Tony going to Tuscany to learn about wine. The coffee was very comforting this morning. We sit down and start our list of questions for Uncle Luca.

"OK, my questions are: Who will pay for travel? Who will make the travel arrangements? Where will I live? Will I have a car? Will I be paid? When will this happen?"

"I think that's a good start. So, will you tell Uncle Luca you want to go to Tuscany?" I ask.

"I thought about it, and I think the answer is yes. I work for a Drywall Contractor now. This would be exciting, new, and fun—an opportunity that may never happen again," Tony shares.

I stand up and grab his hands. He stands, and I give him a huge hug. "I completely agree with you and will support you every step of the way, even though you'll be gone for six months. This relationship will survive." I smile.

"Let's call Uncle Luca and tell him we'll meet him at the restaurant in an hour," Tony says.

When we get to Bertelli's, Uncle Luca is sitting at Tony's favorite table having a cappuccino. *A latte sounds good to me.*

"Hi, Uncle Luca. Good morning. I have been thinking about your offer and am extremely interested, but I have some questions," Tony says.

"Good, Tony," Uncle Luca says.

Angelo walks over. "May I have a latte?" I ask. "Tony, what can I get you?" Angelo asks.

"Just water, thanks."

"Luca, are you OK, or would you like another cappuccino?" Angelo asks.

"I'm fine. Let's get to some of your questions, Tony."

"OK. When will this happen?"

"May through October. This way, you will experience first bud, trim, harvest, crush, fermentation, and bottling." Luca explains.

"Who will pay for travel and make my travel arrangements? Tony asks.

"Me," Luca says. "Next question."

Angelo appears with a latte and water.

"Where will I live?"

"With me, in my villa on the winery property," Luca says.

"Will I have a car?"

"You shouldn't need one, but if you do, you can borrow one of mine," Luca states.

"The last question is, will I be paid?" Tony says.

"Is this a concern for you? Room and board will be in return for your work on the vineyard, so there will be no rent or food bills. Maybe it's pocket money that you're worried about. How about if you accept the offer now, I will throw in $300 a month for your phone and other incidental expenses. How does that sound?" Luca asks.

"I accept!" Tony shouts. "Thank you very much for this opportunity."

"And what about you, young lady?" Luca asks.

"I think he made the right decision, and I will support him every step of the way," I proclaim.

Tony grabs my hand and mouths thank you.

"Now, all we have to do is tell your parents you're going to Tuscany," I say.

16

MONDAY MORNING CAME quickly, as usual, especially after a fantastic weekend like the one we just had. All the way to work, I keep thinking about how Tony is going to Tuscany. He told Maria and Vinnie Sunday night, and they were thrilled. I finally get to the office. I grab a coffee and make my way to Jose's office.

"Good morning; how was your weekend?" I ask Jose as I walk into his office.

"Great, Davis had a baseball game, so that was fun—something to do," Jose says. "How about you?"

"Tony has an Uncle from Tuscany, and we took him wine tasting—what a time!" I say. "What's on tap for this week?"

"I need you to help at the computer with the Miller bid tomorrow. That's about it," Jose explains.

"I'll do whatever you need me to do. Should I get here early tomorrow?" I ask.

"Sure, if you can. The bid is at 2:00 p.m., and it always helps to start getting organized early," Jose says.

"Is there a weekly meeting today?"

"Yes, please join us so you can keep up with what everyone has going on."

I leave Jose's office, get another coffee, and finally sit down in my office and look at my email. There's one from Chip

Harris, wanting to go to lunch today, and one from Kathy Sullivan, asking if I wanted to go to lunch today.

The 9:00 a.m. meeting is starting. Jose, Hank, Kathy, Dan, and I were there, coffee and donuts in front of us.

"Good morning. Let's get started. The Miller bid is on Tuesday at 2:00 p.m. Loretta will be on the computer. I need two more to help with the incoming bids."

"I can round up two volunteers," Hank says.

"This is a call-in bid, so we don't need a bid runner," Jose says. "Kathy, do you have all the forms filled out and the call-in number?"

"Yes. I need to FedEx the forms to Miller today. I need each of you to review them before noon so I have time to revise them if needed before the FedEx pickup today," Kathy states.

Jose says, "Great. We can all meet here at 11:00 a.m. "for lunch. Hank, what do you have going on for the week?"

"I'm meeting with Chevron this Wednesday, and that's it. I'm on vacation next week, so maybe it's a good thing it's slow."

"Dan?"

"We have the Miller bid; that's it," Dan says.

"Kathy?"

"I have a lunch scheduled with Western Pacific Bank on Thursday. I'll take Loretta with me to help with the selling. They have a few projects in the financial district that I'll report back on," Kathy says.

"OK, everyone, have a good week," Jose smiles.

I catch up to Kathy on the way out. "So, I'm going to lunch with you on Thursday, right? Luckily, I'm free," I say.

"I'm sorry. I should have talked to you before announcing it to the group, but I've already talked to you about this. I need help to do my job but rarely get it. So, if you can help me, I'd appreciate it," Kathy says.

"I'm with you. Just let me know what time on Thursday, the dress code, and the means of transportation," I say and walk down the hall to my office.

I sit at my desk and call Chip Harris.

"Hi, this is Chip."

"Hi, this is Loretta. I got your email, and I'd love to go to lunch with you today."

"Super. I'll be outside headquarters at 11:45. See you then," Chip says.

I head to the elevator lobby at 11:35. I think it won't be too bad to hang out on California Street with the cable cars passing, ringing their bells.

Chip pulls up in a two-door Jaguar. I get in and say, "Hi, nice car."

He looks at me like he wants to kiss me and says, "Hi, back. It's great to see you. We are going to the Ramp if that's OK."

"I love the Ramp—nothing fancy there," I share.

The Ramp is a bar and restaurant south of market in San Francisco, right next to a boatyard and on the waterfront, and away from the hustle and bustle of the financial district. We get a seat outside with a view of the boatyard. It is perfect.

"So, Loretta, how do you like working at headquarters?" Chip asks.

"I like it when I have something to do. On a project, you always have something to do," Loretta says. "At headquarters, there are times when you don't have anything to do."

"It's a little slow out there. Banks aren't investing. Companies aren't expanding, and the future business is volatile," Chip reveals.

We order drinks and lunch and relax.

"Are you bidding on the Miller project? I'm working on that tomorrow?" I ask.

"Yes, we are."

"Unlike the last bid I worked on, I know nothing about the job's details. I'm not the lead estimator on the Miller project. I'm just helping in the bid room," I say.

"Are you ready to go?" Chip asks.

"Sure," I say.

He pays the tab, and we collect our stuff to go.

"Good luck tomorrow on the Miller project," I say.

Chip drops me off at headquarters, and I wander up to my office, thinking about what I will do for the rest of the day. I make it back to my office, and Denise walks in.

"Hi, do you have time for a drink after work?" She asks.

"I most certainly do," I say.

"I'll swing by and pick you up around 5:00 p.m."

"Perfect."

Denise leaves, and I sit contemplating the situation. H&S doesn't have much work, and I don't have much to do. Maybe this was the time most people who worked here for years would clean out and organize their files. I don't have hardly any files—in fact, only one—so it won't take me too long to clean out and organize my files. I call Bob Kreft to see if he has anything on the horizon. "I just got off the phone with Kathy. She's asking me the same thing." *Well, she said she needed help.*

Denise calls and says we can leave early. "Thank God," I say. "Anytime works for me."

Denise and I end up at Max's around 4:00. Frank waves, and we shout, "Yes, please," which means "the usual." Denise gets our drinks, and we get settled.

"So, how are you?" I ask.

"I'm fine. Josh is on a rampage. He's usually like this at month end for no apparent reason," Denise states. "How about you?"

"Well, there isn't much going on at headquarters, so I don't have much to do. We're bidding a job tomorrow. I don't know anything about it. I'm just helping with the bid."

"So, how can you help with the bid if you know nothing about the job?" Denise asks.

"I sit at the computer, which has a bid spreadsheet set up, and I input any changes that come in from the subs into the spreadsheet," I explain. "But I have better news. My boyfriend Tony is going to Tuscany, Italy, for six months to learn the wine business from his Uncle Luca."

"Wow, that sounds exciting," Denise says.

"I'm not sure what I'm going to do without him. He's leaving next week."

17

I GET TO work early on Tuesday to set up for the Miller bid. Jose and I layout the bid table and order lunch, and I get more coffee. When I return with two full cups, we sit and relax for a moment. Bid day doesn't allow much relaxing.

"I'm hoping this bid is successful. We need the work," Jose states.

"Is this a job I can project manage?" I ask.

"I don't know. Dan Roberts would be better to answer that question," Jose explains.

We get back to work analyzing bids received this morning. At 11:00 a.m., we get two helpers—*probably there for a free lunch*. Right now, the estimate of the bid is $27.5 million. Getting this job today would be so nice; it could be my next project. Numbers fly across the room as bids come in.

"Where are we at, Loretta?" Jose asks.

"We are at $27.3 million," I say.

"OK, we have fifteen more minutes. Kathy, you have the call-in number? They require nothing else at bid time, correct?"

"No, nothing other than our price," Kathy says.

A few more bids come in. "Loretta, cut $50,000 off electrical."

"That's $7.99 million."

"Three minutes. Where are we?"

"We are at $27.225 million. Kathy, call it in."

We all take a deep breath and look at each other like we just ran a marathon.

"Kathy, when will we know the results?" Jose asks.

"I was told later this afternoon," Kathy says.

"So, I guess we can sit around and wait for a phone call or return to nothing to do."

"I think we should sit around waiting for a phone call," I say. "It will be something to do."

An hour later, the call comes in. H&S got the job! I am so happy; everyone is happy. Dan Roberts has a lot of work to do now.

I need to talk to Dan and see if I'm the project manager of choice. I go down to his office. I poke my head in and say, "Can we talk?"

"Sure, come on in," Dan says.

"I was just wondering if I could be the project manager on the Miller project. I've been off a project for a few months and waiting for the next assignment," I explain.

Dan pauses before he says, "I already picked Bruce to be this project's manager if we are successful."

"Oh," I respond.

"You have been an asset to the estimating department since you've been here. It might be OK if you stay at headquarters for a while," Dan explains.

"That's not what my ambition is. I would prefer to be on the job site and deal with real construction issues," I say.

I get up and leave Dan's office with a little attitude.

I drive home and get to T's with a purpose. I have a lot to tell her. She opens the door and says, "There you are! I've been wondering where you've been. Come on in."

As I walk in, T rushes to get a bottle of wine. I sit down and wait for her to return. The view from her house is so spectacular that it makes waiting a pleasure. She returns with two glasses of wine and sits next to me.

"So, what has been going on?" T asks.

"Tony is going to Tuscany, Italy, for six months to learn the wine business from his Uncle Luca. How cool is that?"

"WHAT, that's fabulous," T says.

"How are you and Cal?" I ask.

"We're fine. We are planning a vacation to Jackson Hole for the summer. We're looking forward to it. So, where's your next project?" T asks.

"I don't know. It's scary not knowing. We got a job today. I asked the operations manager if I could manage it, but he had already chosen someone else," I say. "He said I should be happy in the estimating department. Last I checked, you never want anyone to know you are good at estimating because they will never want you to leave."

T laughs. I stand up and say, "I should go home." T stands and hugs me. "Thanks for stopping by. Let's go to the yacht club in the next few days."

"That sounds great."

18

I'M NOT REALLY in the mood for work today. I thought I had a chance at that job. It's a seismic upgrade in San Francisco to an existing historical building near Union Square. It has my name all over it. Now, with little to do at the office, I can concentrate on Tony's departure. Tonight is his going away dinner at Bertelli's. I asked Jose if I could leave a little early to attend the party. He smiles and agrees that it's OK for such an important event. I thank him and tell him I'll see him tomorrow.

I am so excited to see Tony. I pull into the parking lot at Bertelli's and get the last space. I jump out of the car and hurry into the restaurant. At this point, I'm only looking for one person. I finally see him standing, talking to his cousins. They are probably wondering why Uncle Luca picked him and not one of them. I make my way in that direction.

"You're here!" Tony shouts. He runs over and gives me a big hug and kiss.

"Hi, this is so exciting. Are you doing OK?" I ask.

"I'm fine. Mom and Dad are a little stressed. Uncle Luca left yesterday. He'll have two days to prepare for my arrival," Tony explains.

"Are you packed and ready to go?" I ask.

"Sort of. I don't know what to bring," Tony admits.

"He said you'll work in the vineyard, so bring some work clothes. You might be working in the winery making wine and serving wine, so bring some nicer stuff. I'd bring some shorts and play stuff. You never know. Does that help?" I ask.

"It does. Thanks. Let's go find a seat and get something to drink," Tony says.

I smile and follow him. I see Maria and Vinnie sitting at Tony's favorite table, where Tony stops and says, "Let's sit with my Mom and Dad."

I sit down and say, "Hi, Maria. Hi, Vinnie. How are you?"

"This is something that we never thought would happen. We are both very excited for Tony. Maybe we can even visit while he's there," Maria says.

"Are you going to visit, Lolly?" Vinnie asks.

"I don't know. We really didn't talk about it. It all happened so fast," I say.

Tony arrives with wine and glasses. "I hope she visits, and you, too, Mom and Dad," Tony smiles.

Vinnie gets up from the table and stands front and center. "Hi, everyone. Thanks for coming. Before we start dinner, I just want to say a few words. Uncle Luca is a big part of this family. His CalaLuca winery in Tuscany is a big part of our family. Maria and I are very thankful to Luca for giving Tony this opportunity, and we are proud of our son, Tony, for accepting his offer. We wish you the best of luck on this learning experience. Congratulations, Tony. We all love you very much and wish you well."

Everyone applauds to congratulate Tony, knowing dinner will be served soon.

I have tears in my eyes listening to Vinnie. My heart is sinking with the thought of Tony leaving. I'll try to keep a happy face on tonight. I'm sure there will be more tears later.

Dinner is served—your choice of spaghetti or lasagna. It is all wonderful. Tony fills everyone's glasses with wine. He has the biggest smile on his face. We start eating, and I ask, "How did Hard Drywall react to your request for a leave of absence?"

"I didn't ask for a leave of absence; I resigned," Tony explains.

"Oh, so how did they react to your resignation?" I ask. "What are they going to do?"

"I told them my plans, and they gave me a high five and said good luck!" Tony says.

You gotta love contractors. "What about your house?" I ask.

"My cousin is going to sublease from me while I'm gone. I think it's a win-win situation," Tony says.

"And your truck?"

"Vinnie's going to park it at his house. He's got the room," Tony answers.

"And one last question: who is taking you to the airport tomorrow?"

"Maria and Vinnie. I'll drive over tomorrow and jump in their vehicle. I'll leave them the keys in case they have to move it. It works perfectly."

I smile, no more questions. Actually, I have a few more, but I'll ask Tony in private. The crowd is talking and laughing and having a good time. I'm happy for Tony and that he has this much support from his family.

"I thought of another question. Sorry. What time is your flight tomorrow?" I ask.

"It leaves at 10:00 a.m. I'll land at 8:00 a.m. the following day. Uncle Luca is going to pick me up at the airport."

"Do you have a passport? I promise that's my last question."

"Yes, expedited at Marin County Admin two days ago. Do you want to come over to my house tonight?" Tony asks.

"I would love to. I know you have a few things going on, but I have six months of cuddling to do in one night, plus giving you a proper sendoff. That's OK, right?"

"Absolutely. Sounds like we might have to start this cuddling and proper sendoff sooner than later," Tony says.

"OK, let's go!" I cheer.

Tony said his goodbyes, threw kisses to everyone, and walked out the door with me by his side. When we arrive at his house, it looks like I will help him pack.

"Can I help you fold and put stuff in the suitcase?" I ask.

"Yes, please. I'm very distracted. I have to leave at 7:00 a.m. to go to Maria and Vinnie's; the airport is an hour-and-a-half drive. That will get me there at 8:30 a.m. I think that's plenty of time, but it's not like I know the international flight process," Tony says.

"You'll be fine. Let's get these clothes in these suitcases and start cuddling," I smile. "I have to work in the morning."

Tony grabs me, hugs me, and says, "Thanks, I will miss you." He has no idea how much I'm going to miss him.

19

IT'S FRIDAY THE thirteenth. That's a bad luck day if you're superstitious. I get to the office in record time since it's Friday. Tony got to Tuscany yesterday. He checked in to tell me how fabulous CalaLuca Winery is and how nice his accommodations are. After one day, he said it had exceeded his expectations. He'll keep me posted.

I try to settle in my office, but all I'm doing is staring out the window at the building next door, across the alley. Last night was the perfect send-off for Tony, both at the restaurant and at his house. I smile, thinking about it, when my phone rings.

"H&S, this is Loretta."

"Hi, this is Dan. Can you come down to my office?"

"Now?" I ask.

"Yes, if you have a minute," Dan says.

"I'll be right there," I respond.

I grab my coffee cup, stop by the coffee room, and fill it up. I don't have a clue what Dan wants to talk about. Maybe he changed his mind and wants me to be the project manager of the Miller project. I'll soon find out. I knock on the door of his office.

"Hi, Loretta. Come in, and can you close the door behind you?" Dan asks.

"Yes," I say as I close the door and sit at his desk.

"I don't know how to say this other than just saying it. We have to lay you off, Loretta—effective today. We have very little work, and as a company, we have to stay above water," Dan explains.

I am numb. I think I heard what he said, but I'm not sure. It's not like I want to ask him to say it again. *You are laid off!* Of course, I heard him.

"Loretta, you're not saying much. Do you have any questions?" Dan asks.

"Why me? Who else is getting let go?" I ask.

"Well, for one thing, you don't have an assigned project to work on, and you are a female." He looks at me and winks. "We are keeping the male project managers for any future work we get," Dan states.

Now, I'm numb. I can feel my blood pressure rising, and I'm getting angry. *And we all know what happens when I'm angry. I cry.* I stand up, pick up my coffee cup, and leave Dan's office. My eyes are filling with tears. I can't control it. I walk into the coffee room on the way back to my office. Jose is getting a cup of coffee. He takes one look at me and asks, "Are you OK?"

"No, I am not OK. Dan just laid me off. He said he's letting me go because I'm female, and he's keeping his male project managers," I cry.

"Get a coffee and come down to my office," Jose says. "This is the first I've heard about this, and you technically work for me," Jose states.

I follow him to his office, and he closes the door. *Jose never closes his door.* I think Jose is just as pissed as I am.

"So, this just happened?"

"Yes, he called and asked if I could come to his office," I explain. "He said it was effective today, which means I wake up today with a job and go home without one. He said he's not laying off anyone else. I'm the only one," I cry, tears running down my face.

"Did he say anything about severance pay or compensation to you?" Jose asks.

"No."

"You've helped me out tremendously since you've been here. I don't want you to be laid off, but I'll be honest with you; the operation managers have more pull around here than me, and it doesn't help that Hank is on vacation this week. You have to wonder if that wasn't planned," Jose admits. "I can't help you at this moment, but I can see if anybody is hiring and try to help you find a new position soon. I guess you'll have to pack your office up by the end of the day. I'll come and check on you later."

"Thanks, Jose," I smile—sort of. I leave his office and return to mine. I sit down and think, *Oh my God, what will I do? I have bills to pay and no one else to rely on for money. H&S compensates for gas and a car allowance. I'm on my own for that now. I love working for H&S, and I guess I was wrong to think I was doing a great job. The company loyalty only goes one way, and that's up.* I sit and try to calm down, and the phone rings.

"Hi, H&S, this is Loretta."

"Hi, this is Chip. How are you?"

"Not good. I got laid off today, so I don't work here anymore," I cry.

"Well, I tell you what. I'll pick you up in twenty minutes to take you out for lunch and cocktails to make you feel a little better. How does that sound?" Chip asks.

"Sounds like just what I need. Thanks. I'll be outside in twenty minutes."

Chip pulls up just as I walk out of headquarters. I get in his car with tears in my eyes. He hugs me as soon as sit down, which helps a lot. I look into his eyes and say, "I'm a wreck."

"We'll fix you up in no time. How about Sinbad's? There's lots of parking. We can sit at the bar, get drunk, and eat. What do you say?"

"Perfect."

We pull into the parking lot at Sinbad's. It's right on the bay front with great views. I'm still a wreck. I hope I can hold myself together enough to get into the restaurant. I'm feeling weak. We sit at the bar, and Chip orders two shots of tequila.

"I told you I was going to make you feel better," Chip says. "You have to tell me what happened. I was very surprised. I didn't know H&S was laying people off."

"Well, I got called into the ops manager's office this morning and was told I no longer have a job. I asked him why, and he said because I was female like he was joking, but he wasn't," I say as my eyes tear up again.

We both shoot our shots of tequila.

"Wow, that might make me feel better," I say. "It is Friday, the thirteenth—a great day for the executives of H&S to say, 'It's Friday the thirteenth. Let's lay off some people today!'"

I continued, "We should eat something. I have to go and pack up my office when I get back, and I didn't tell anyone in the office about this. Management didn't tell anyone in the office about it, either." I say.

We order another drink and some food and look at the time. Who cares? I don't work anymore.

We order another drink and look at each other.

"Are you OK?" Chip asks.

"I'm a little tipsy, but I think what happened today is sinking in. I loved working for H&S. When I walk out of the office today, I don't ever want to go back. It's like a divorce. You are told it's over by your spouse, and you just sit there and think, what? I've never been divorced, or married for that matter, but if you love something or someone, and then, one day, you are told you have to leave, it must feel the same way."

Chip pays the bill, and we hold on to each other, walking out of Sinbad's. It's 3:00 p.m., and I stagger to my office and sit down. Minutes later, Denise walks in and says, "What the hell is going on? I was told to cut your checks and deliver them to you. What did you do wrong?"

"Shut the door. Do you have a minute?" I ask.

"Yes. What did he say to you? Did you do something wrong?" Denise asks.

"I didn't do anything wrong, by the way. At least, I don't think I did. Dan called me to his office and asked me to shut the door. *Unless something is wrong, no one ever shuts their office doors around here.* He told me I was being laid off because there is no work. All I felt was a slap across my face and heard leave now, " I cry. "I can't believe Hank isn't here. Jose knew nothing about it."

"You don't think Hank knew?" Denise asks.

"I don't know. He probably did. What do I know?" I say.

"Do you want me to help you pack up?" Denise asks.

"No, I don't have that much stuff. What I do need is a box," I say.

"I can do that for you. I'll be right back," Denise states.

"Thanks," I smile. It's 3:30 p.m. If I sit down, I'll cry, so I poke my head into Jose's office. He looks up and hurries around his desk, ensuring I'm alright.

"Hi, I got my checks, and Denise is getting me a box to take away my personal stuff. I don't have much. I just wanted to say goodbye."

"Shut the door and sit down," Jose requests.

"I talked to Barry Bailey, the president of Bevis, Inc. He said he is hiring. H&S is working with them on several projects. Their offices are in Oakland. Barry told me to give you his number and have you call him when you get a chance," Jose states.

"Thanks, Jose. It might be a few days before I bounce back and want to speak to anyone. *It's definitely going to take a couple of days.*

Denise returns with a box and says goodbye. I pack up and tell everyone I see on the way out to "have a nice weekend." It could be a long drive home.

20

I'M A MESS. I've never felt this way, and it doesn't feel good. There has always been control, planning, execution, and reward to everything I do. I am sitting here, in my triplex, staring out the windows at the City, the bridges, and the sailboats, trying to make sense of what just happened to me. I think I need a place to forget what just happened. I can't think of anywhere I would rather be. It's beautiful and quiet, but I'm still a mess. I don't know what I need—well, besides a job.

I have no family here. I never have. I was born in Pittsburgh, Pennsylvania. After graduating from the University of Pittsburgh, I accepted a job in California and moved here alone. You need self-confidence to do that, and I had a job. Now, I don't have self-confidence or a job!

If someone asked why they should hire me, I'd probably say, "I don't know. The last company laid me off. I don't know if you should hire me." How does someone get self-esteem and self-confidence? I have always had it, but I don't have it right now. I have to get it back before I search for a job, or I'll never get one.

I get the energy to go to the yacht club. I don't know if it's a good idea. I don't know if I want to talk about this or not. I can pretend I'm fine, have a cocktail, leave, or tell everyone what happened and recover a little.

I walk into the yacht club, straight to my favorite bar stool, and sit down. Charles walks over. "Hi, Lolly. Long time no see," he says as he brings me a Zinfandel.

"Hi, Charles. How are you?"

"I'm fine. How are you? *This is decision time. I can lie or tell him what's really going on.*

"I got laid off today," I say. "I'm not doing too good."

"Oh, that's not right. Are you OK?

"No. I'm a mess," I say. "It's Friday the thirteenth. How can a company, in their right mind, lay someone off on Friday the thirteenth? If you let me just sit here and listen to all the bar chatter, I think it will help. I don't want to go home right now and be alone."

Charles looks at me, smiles, and walks away to help another member. I just stare across the bar, looking to see if I recognize anybody. Friday nights at the yacht club used to be happening. Everyone who lived here started here on Friday nights, but we never finished here. We always finished ordering pizza, Chinese, or barbecue at someone's house. No one had far to go home. We could all stagger home at a reasonable hour. I didn't recognize anyone. *I don't think a lot of us live here anymore.* I wave to Charles and say, "Yes, please."

Charles returns to my seat, full glass in hand, and asks, "How are you doing?"

"A little better. Can I ask you a question?"

"Let me get a beer and join you. I can get up if I get a customer," Charles says.

I take a slow sip of wine and wait for Charles to return. He sits down and asks, "So what's the question?"

"Well, I'm trying to figure out how I feel about this whole 'I don't have a job' thing. I used to have a lot of self-confidence, but they took that away from me today when they slapped me across the face and said, 'Get out, now.' To start looking for a new job, I need some self-confidence. So, the question is, do you know how to regain self-confidence? You seem self-confident behind the bar and in interacting with the members. I thought maybe you could advise me on how to get it back—and fast," I explain.

Charles looks around like he's thinking and asks, "Did you feel comfortable with what you did at that company as an employee? Did you do anything wrong that led to you getting laid off?"

"No. I was feeling positive about my work and the relationships I was building. *The most important thing a project manager can do is develop a relationship with the clients, architects, and subcontractors.* No one told me I did anything wrong. They just said, 'Get out Now.'"

"Well, my advice to you is to say out loud, 'They are a bunch of jackasses.' It will make you feel better. Next, use your existing self-confidence, which I know you have some in there, somewhere, to ignore that this feels like it was deliberate and directed at you, ignore what they said to you, and focus on all the good things that come out of the whole experience of working for this company. I know how much you liked working for H&S. Next, think of how much better the next experience will be," Charles shares.

"The sooner you can put this behind you and start moving on to the next thing, the sooner you will feel your self-confidence return, and I said start moving on to the next thing. That may take a while, but don't let that distract you. You may have to fake your confidence early on. It will build over time and come back sooner than you think," Charles explains.

"I'm not good at faking anything," I say. "I'm not a good salesman, even when selling myself."

"So," Charles says, "At your first interview, ask them more questions about their company than they ask you about yourself."

"I like that idea. Thanks for talking to me. This has calmed me down so much. It still may take a couple of days to feel whole again, but I feel like I'm already on the right track with your advice. Thank you."

"You're welcome. Drive safely on the way home," Charles smiles.

21

IT'S SATURDAY, AND I really wish Tony was here. I could use a shoulder to lay my crumbled head on right now. However, there's a nine-hour difference between here and Tuscany, which means it's 7:00 p.m. there. Hopefully, he's done working and relaxing for the day. I dial my phone, and he picks up.

"Lolly, you must be reading my mind. I was just about to call you. I just had a weird feeling about you and wanted to make sure you were all right," Tony says. "Is everything OK?"

"No. I got laid off yesterday from H&S. I'm a mess. You know that I loved working for them, and for them to tell me to leave was like a slap in my face. I wish you were here to make me feel better," I say.

"Oh, Lolly, I wish I was there, too. I'm still in shock. I can't believe they'd do that to you," Tony states.

"And on Friday the thirteenth! Talk about bad luck," I share. "I don't think I can get through an interview with another company right now. I have a lead with Bevis, Inc. Jose said they were hiring, and I should call the president."

"Maybe you can take advantage of this and take a little time off. Did they give you severance pay?" Tony asks.

"Yes, two weeks plus unused vacation, which is about four weeks," I explain.

"See, that's what I mean. Just calm down. You have time to think about your next move. You don't have to take the first offer that comes," Tony says.

"The first thing, in my mind, was I need a job—now. Thanks for putting that in perspective. I might be able to think about my next move, what I want, and what I think I deserve," I say.

"Exactly," Tony says. "That's why I love you."

"I love you and miss you, too," I smile. "How's Uncle Luca?

"He's great. I enjoy working for him. He's got a special place here now, and I'm a part of it. One day, you may be a part of it, too." Tony says.

"I knew talking to you would make me feel much better. Thank you. Thank you."

"I'll call you tomorrow. You are going to be fine. I'm sure of it," Tony says.

I hang up, and I have one last call. I have to let T know what's going on. I dial her number, but she doesn't answer. I leave a message to call me back when she gets a chance. Maybe Cal is in town. It is Saturday. He's usually here on the weekends. I make another cup of coffee, sit on the couch, and stare at the bay, the City, Mt. Tam, the bridges, the sailboats and tankers, and the clouds and sun. The phone rings, interrupting my thoughts. I was in a trance, but that's gone now.

"Hello."

"Hi, it's Trisha. What's going on?"

"Hi. Are you home?" I ask.

"Yes, Cal should be here in a few hours, so I went grocery shopping for food for the weekend. What about you?" T asks.

"I'm home, but I'm not thrilled to be alone right now. Can I come up, or can you come down?" I ask.

"You OK?" T asks.

"No, but I want to tell you this in person," I explain.

"Why don't you come up, and how do Bloody Marys sound?" T asks.

"Great. I'll be up in ten minutes."

I go downstairs and put on some shorts and a sweatshirt. I walk out the front door, which is rare for me, lock it, and walk up the half block to T's house. I knocked on the door, but she opened it almost immediately. T runs toward me to make sure I'm OK.

"You got me nervous on the phone. Come on in. Bloody's are ready to go," T says.

"Thanks for letting me come over," I say. I walk in and sit down at the table by the window with the view. This view never gets old. T brings over the drinks, sits down, and says, "Spit it out. You're killing me with suspense."

"Let me take a sip of Bloody Mary first. Let's cheers because we're together," I smile. We cheers with our glasses and take a sip. "I got laid off yesterday."

"Oh, God. I thought you were going to tell me you or Tony got hurt or something. Those bastards. How dare they lay you off?" T screams. "I want details."

"Well, I got called into Dan's office, the operations manager for the building group. I really don't know this guy; I only met him twice. He called me into his office and said to close the door and sit down. Then he said, 'We are going to have to lay you off, Loretta—effective today.' I asked him why me and who else was getting let go. Dan said, 'Well, for one thing, you don't have an assigned project to work on, and you are a female.' He looked at me, winked, and said, 'We are keeping the male project managers for any future work we get.' I got so angry that I stood up and left his office."

"I'd sue them. He really said you don't have an assigned project, and you are female, and we are keeping the male project managers for future projects?" T asks.

"Yes."

"That's not right—not in this day and age. Women have a role in every business and operation," T explains.

"Listen to you; you sound like a women's rights advocate. I'm just a project manager trying to do my job. I can't sue them. I love this company," I say.

"After what they just did to you? They just broke up with you and demanded a divorce. They told you to get out in eight hours, not a month—eight hours. They want you to establish relationships with your clients, architects, and subcontractors, but they establish this kind of relationship with their employees. Yes, you can," T says. "Let's not talk about it right now. Let's talk about you. How are you?"

"I'm a train wreck. I never have not had a job. Chip, a subcontractor I work with, took me for lunch and cocktails Friday to try and ease the pain. I ended up at the yacht club and had a great inspirational talk with Charles last night, and I talked to Tony this morning in Italy. He's doing great and told me to take some time off and that I didn't need to find a job tomorrow. It was great advice," I say as I take a sip of Bloody Mary.

"So, now what? You just need to relax for a few days, shopping and sailing. I know you don't like shopping, so why don't I set up a booze cruise for tomorrow? Getting you out on the bay will do magic for your soul. What do you think?" T asks.

"I agree. Sometimes, when I'm on the bay, it feels like I am thousands of miles away," I say. "Anything I can do to help?"

"I'll invite Brian and Steve and pick up some beer." Just as I stand to refill our drinks, Cal storms through the door.

T runs to greet him. "Hi, honey. Welcome home. Lolly is here. She needed some company. She got laid off yesterday."

Cal comes over and gives me a big hug. I haven't seen him in a few weeks. "Those rat bastards. I'd sue them. You, of all people—one of the best project managers I've ever worked with," Cal says.

"Thanks, Cal."

T returns with refills, and Cal joins us. "I should probably leave you two alone as soon as I finish my drink," I say.

"So, Cal, how do you like Fresno?" I ask.

"Fresno is a horrible little town. We are building a manufacturing facility for Skechers, and I have two more weeks to go. Then, I'll be back here for good," Cal says.

"So, are you moving in with T?" I ask.

"Maybe, maybe not. We'll have to talk about it. I don't know," Cal says.

I finish my drink, stand up, and say, "I'm going to go home and leave you two lovebirds alone. Thank you for the support and the drinks. Call me about sailing tomorrow. I'm looking forward to it."

I give them hugs and walk home.

22

IT'S SATURDAY AFTERNOON. I open a bottle of wine, pour a glass, and walk out onto the deck. It's a fabulous, sunny, warm day, and there's not a cloud in the sky. There are hundreds of boats sailing. Maybe there is a regatta in progress. I sit here, still recovering from what happened, watching the sailboats, sipping some wine by myself. I think of what T and Cal said.

I should sue them. I never thought of that. I thought I just had to put my tail between my legs, head down, and walk out the door as instructed. I guess I never thought about how hurt and humiliated I am, which is purely the result of the layoff. They did little to assist in the aftermath. I was offered no support, no counseling, and no further discussion. I was asked to leave—end of discussion.

What does Hank think of this? I don't even know if he knows. I know Jose didn't know I was getting laid off. I feel so alone at H&S about this. You don't get a going away party when you're laid off. I didn't even say goodbye to the people I worked with every day. They probably think that's rude of me now that they found out I no longer work there. I take another sip of wine and stare at the Golden Gate Bridge, trying to put some of my thoughts into perspective.

Finally, I get up, empty wine glass in hand, and head to the kitchen. The phone rings. "Hello."

"Hi, it's Trisha. Sail is set up on Foghead for tomorrow at 11:00 a.m. The weather should be great. Maybe no foul-weather gear will be required."

"Thanks, T," I say. "See you tomorrow."

I hang up the phone, pour another glass of wine, and return to the deck. I start thinking again. I have to stand up for myself when it comes to companies deciding whether I have a job. However, on the other hand, the company is responsible for hiring and firing employees, whether the employees like it or not. I really don't think I can sue H&S. It's just not me. I'm the type to just walk down the road without looking back. If I did sue H&S, I'd be known as the project manager who sues general contractors.

I am at the yacht club at 10:30 on Sunday morning. I didn't pack my sailing bag for racing; we're booze cruising. T and Cal pull in right after I get out of my car.

"Hi, can I help with anything?" I ask.

"You can carry a bag of snacks to the boat. I don't know if Brian or Steve are here. Let's walk to the boat together and figure it out," T says.

We all walk over to the guest berth that Foghead is in. We climb aboard and out pop Brian and Steve from below.

"Hi, Trisha. Hi, Lolly," Steve says with a smile.

"This is Cal. I don't think you guys know each other," T says.

"Hi, I'm Steve. This is Brian."

"And I'm Cal."

"Welcome aboard, Cal," Brian says. The plan is to sail to Tiberon and have lunch at the San Francisco Yacht Club. Lolly gets reciprocal membership from the East Marin Yacht Club, and it's a really nice place."

Steve starts the motor as we untie from the berth. He maneuvers out of the berth and heads for the bay. Just before reaching the shipping channel, T hoists the main. The marina is behind us now, and nothing but San Francisco Bay is ahead.

Brian hoists a small jib within about five minutes, and Steve cuts the motor. It is very quiet as we sail through the waves. This will soothe my soul. No one is talking; we're just soaking it all in—the City, the bridges, and the Marin headlands.

I close my eyes and feel the breeze on my face, washing away the last few days. It's so relaxing on the bay. We're fast approaching Tiburon, so Steve, as skipper, tells Trisha to drop the jib. I release the halyard on the mainsail, which collects on the deck. T and I fold it, preparing it for our return.

Guest berths at the SFYC are empty, so we can float into the perfect spot. T jumps to the dock and secures Foghead to the cleats. We all jump to the dock and head to the yacht club. I had to check in with someone before we could be seated. It must have worked because we got seated at a table for five on the deck with a bay view of Belvedere Island, the City, and the Golden Gate Bridge.

"Hi, how is everyone this afternoon? Can I get you started with something to drink?"

T says, "Sure, and what's your name?"

"Annie."

"OK, Annie. To get started, we'll take a pitcher of gin fizzes for five and some lunch menus."

"Coming right up," Annie says and returns to the bar.

"So, Cal, have you been here before?" I ask.

"No, what an amazing spot. Lolly, how are you feeling today?" Cal asks.

"Better, but it's going to take a week or two for me to recover a bit, which is exactly what I'm going to do. I plan to take some time off before I try to find another job."

"What are you going to do?" Steve asks.

"Absolutely nothing and we all know that when we say we have absolutely nothing to do, we are busier than ever," I say.

"Maybe you should take a vacation," T suggests. "That might bring this all together for you."

"I've never been on vacation by myself, but the more I think about it, the more I agree that it might help tremendously," I state.

Annie brings the pitcher of gin fizzes and menus. We have all afternoon, so we all cheers our drinks and look at the menu. The gin fizzes are perfect. Annie returns and takes our orders, and we add another pitcher of fizzes as well.

Lunch is served. We enjoy the food, the fizzes, and the time getting to know each other better. I settle up with the SFYC, and we head back to EMYC. We use the same berth we left, tidy the boat, collect the garbage, and head to the yacht club. We all look like we've been sailing but not racing.

As soon as I open the door, I hear, "Lolly, come on in!" It's Charles. We walk up to the bar. Everyone knows Charles, so there's no need for introductions.

"Yes, please."

"And how are you feeling today?"

"Trisha arranged a cruise to the San Francisco Yacht Club, where we had lunch and gin fizzes. You make better gin fizzes, by the way. It was a fantastic afternoon. Booze cruising is good for your head."

Charles retrieves the other drinks, and we sit down.

"Thanks so much for today. I needed it," I smile.

"I'm glad. I was so worried about you yesterday," T says.

23

I GRAB COFFEE and sit on the deck overlooking the City and bay. The idea of a vacation is growing on me. If I think about what I would like to do on vacation, it would be to sit by a pool in a warm climate with little chance of rain, eat at nice restaurants, and give myself time to think about forgetting about what just happened and focus on what I want in the future.

Maybe Hawaii would be a perfect place to land for a few days and start working on that self-confidence that I was looking for. I grab the phone and call T.

"Hello."

"This is Lolly. Good morning. I hope I didn't wake you."

"No, we've been up for hours," T says.

"Do you want to go to Hawaii with me?" I ask.

"WHAT?!" T asks.

"I decided I want to go to Hawaii for a week, and the thought of going alone doesn't thrill me, so I thought I'd at least ask."

"I think you going on vacation is a great idea, but I'm not going to have the time to join you," T explains.

"I figured I'd ask, and it's OK," I say.

"You'll have a great time by yourself. Just think of all the people you'll meet. Maybe you'll find a job there and not come home," T screams.

"That's a possibility, but I'd rather relax there and come home ready to get a job," I respond.

"When are you leaving?" T asks.

"I haven't even tried to book or plan a trip," I reveal. "I'll let you know when I'm leaving. It will be in the next six weeks."

* * *

I booked a flight from Oakland, CA, to Maui, HI, the next day. I leave Monday at 10:00 a.m. and return the following Monday. I also reserve a room at the Maui Marriott Resort for six days. I reserve a space at the Park 'N Fly at the Oakland Airport. So, that gives me five days to pack and eat all the meat and veggies in the refrigerator. I don't have to shop for clothes because I don't have a job. I'll wear what I have, even if it's not Hawaiian shirts and Tommy Bahama sun dresses.

I'm getting excited. Hawaii is beautiful, so it's the perfect place to sit by the pool or on the beach and do nothing. The temperature is perfect in the morning, noon, and night. The only thing I have to do before I go is tell T and Charles I'm going. It's not like I have anyone at work to tell. I'll call Denise when I get back.

Saturday rolls around, and I call T.
"Hello."
"Hi, it's Lolly. How are you?"
"I'm fine. What's up?"
"I'm leaving for Hawaii for a week on Monday. I was going to hang out at the yacht club this afternoon. Want to go?"
"I can't. Cal and I are going furniture shopping since he'll be here for a while starting today, but stop by for happy hour tomorrow for an appropriate sendoff," T says.

"OK. I'll see you tomorrow," I smile.

I leave for the yacht club around 3:00 p.m. Saturdays are usually slow. What a difference there is in me from a week ago, and it's all because of Charles. His little talk helped me a lot.

I walk into the bar, and Charles is watching the baseball game on his little six-inch TV behind the bar. He doesn't even look up.

"Yes, please," I say. That gets his attention.

"Lolly, how are you? I've been worried about you," Charles says.

"I'm doing much better than the last time you saw me, thanks to you," I explain. "I thought I'd hang out with you today and keep you company." Charles delivers a glass of wine, pulls up his bar stool behind the bar, and pours himself a beer.

"Is the game over?" I ask.

"Bottom of the eighth. The As are getting killed ten to two. It's over. Talk to me. How are you?" Charles asks.

"I'm going to Hawaii on Monday for a week. A few people convinced me I don't have to get a new job tomorrow, and I can take my time figuring out my next move," I explain.

"I think that's a great idea. What island are you going to?" Charles asks.

"Maui."

"Well, the Lahaina Yacht Club reciprocates with us, so you can go there for drinks or dinner at half the price of the restaurants in town," Charles informs me.

"That sounds fantastic. Since I don't have a job, I can't see myself going to expensive places. I'll remember to bring my membership card," I say.

"What are you going to do when you get there?" Charles asks.

"Nothing. I'm going alone, and without the self-confidence I used to have, I plan to lay low and stay close to the resort. What have you been up to?" I ask.

"My birthday's coming up, and Gale and I are going to take a short road trip up the coast. Do you want another?" Charles asks.

"Yes, please."

24

FLIGHT 426 IS boarding at gate seven. I made it after a long happy hour at T's yesterday, a commuter-traffic drive to the airport, and an airport-security experience from hell. I got a window seat. I love sitting in the window seat so I can see where I'm going. I realize that you are over the Pacific Ocean for most of the five-and-a-half-hour flight from Oakland to Maui, and it's the most boring window seat you can get. I don't mind because I brought a book to read. Landing in Maui is one of the most stunning views from a plane I've ever seen. I'm grateful for the window seat.

I arrived at the Maui Marriott Resort. "Hi, I'm here to check-in. My name is Loretta Novak."

"Aloha. Welcome to Hawaii. Let me get you checked in," the reservation gal says.

It is 5:00 p.m. Hawaii time. I get my luggage to the room and head straight to the beach. When I get back to the pool, they have a fabulous outdoor tiki bar that I settle into.

"Can I get you something, Miss?"

"Yes, I'll take a Mai Tai," I say.

As the bartender wanders off to get my drink, I look around and notice everyone is a little younger than me, and everyone is with someone else. I'm here alone. I knew it would be weird by myself, but maybe that's my self-confidence-building exercise. The Mai Tai arrives, and it's better than I expected.

"Welcome to Hawaii," the bartender says.

"Thank you. Do you work here every afternoon?" I ask.

"Yes."

"What's your name?" I ask.

"Myles."

"Thanks, Myles. I'll be here all week, so I'll surely see you again."

I carry my drink to the beach and call Tony. I don't have a clue what time it is in Tuscany, but I'm calling anyway. It goes to voicemail. "Hi, sweetie, I made it to Hawaii. I'm not sure what I will do all week, but I'm sure it will help my head. I miss you. Call me. Love you. Lolly."

I head back to the room and start getting ready. I decided to go to the Lahaina Yacht Club tonight for dinner. The hotel desk arranged transportation, and I arrived at the yacht club with my East Marin Yacht Club card. I walk in the door, and only a few people are in the club.

"Hi, can I help you?"

"Hi, my name is Lolly Novak. I'm an East Marin Yacht Club member and was told I can come here, just like I'm at home."

"Aloha, Lolly, and welcome to the Lahaina Yacht Club. We love the East Marin Yacht Club. Can I get you something to drink?"

"I'll take a Rum Punch, and what is your name?" I ask.

"Zak. I'll get your drink, and we can get acquainted."

Zak returns with my Rum Punch and sits with me at the bar. "So, what brings you to Maui?"

"I needed a refresh on my career," I answer. "I've only been here one day, so I don't know if it's working."

"Well, you are welcome here any time. You just remember that we are your friends."

"Thank you so much. I was worried about coming here by myself, and the staff at the hotel can only make you feel like everybody else."

I take a sip of Rum Punch and ask, "What's up with the ties on the wall?"

"Well, the Lahaina Yacht Club does not allow formal shirts and ties, so if anyone walks in with a tie on, the tie gets cut in half and stuck on the wall. We're casual around here."

"I'm glad you like my yacht club here. I'll stay for dinner and go out on the deck overlooking the ocean."

Zak gets me set up out on the deck. Dinner is fabulous. I just need to say thanks and goodbye and find transportation back to the Marriott. One stop at the bar for a Rum Punch to go, and it's back to the room. I settle on the balcony, and the phone rings.

"Hello."

"Hi, Lolly. How are you?"

"Hi, Tony. I miss you. How are you?" I ask.

"Well, we racked twenty barrels today. It's just part of the process. I never knew it was this complicated, but I'm learning how to do it, so that's a good thing. How is Hawaii?" Tony asks.

"So far, so good. I went to the Lahaina Yacht Club for dinner and met Zak, the bartender, who took care of me. During dinner, I started thinking about what I want to do in my next job and if I want to sue H&S."

"Sue H&S? Where is this coming from?" Tony asks.

"T and Cal said they thought it was something I should think about, so I am," I say. "It's no big deal."

"I hope you're not forgetting how much you loved working for that company," Tony says.

"Their comments took me back, but they are only saying that in my best interest," I say. "What time is it there? It's 7:00 p.m. here."

"It's 7:00 a.m. here. I'm always up at this time and headed to work, but I wanted to talk to you first," Tony says.

"Well, get to work. You don't want to upset Uncle Luca. Tell him I said hi," I reply.

"OK, Lolly. I'll call you later." Tony says and hangs up.

I sit on the balcony, Rum Punch in hand, staring out at the ocean. It's nice, warm, and quiet. Suddenly, I hear drums—loud drums and lots of them. "Aloha!" someone screams across the lawn. It's the nightly luau—so much for my quiet sit on the balcony.

The next several days fly by and include lots of pool time, a few walks on the beach, and a sunset cruise on a huge catamaran. *I love being on the water.* I take another trip to the yacht club, and my last night includes dinner at Longi's for macadamia-nut-covered Mahi Mahi. I arrange for transportation to the airport through the hotel desk and wander over to the bar for a nightcap on my last night here.

"Hi, Myles. How are you tonight?" I ask.

"I'm fine. What can get you?" Myles asks.

"I'll take a Mai Tai," I reply.

As Myles turns to make the drink, I wonder if my mission was accomplished in Hawaii. I still don't know what I want to do and where I want to work, but I do know I don't want to sue H&S for laying me off. In fact, I did a great job of putting the whole thing behind me. I can say I don't want to think about them anymore. Then, I can move on, and I'm ready for that. My self-confidence is back.

Myles sets the drink down, and I smile at him. Just then, a man sits next to me. Myles, standing right next to me, takes his order and rushes off. The man looks at me and says, "Hello."

"Hi, I recognize you from the pool and the sunset cruise. My name is Lolly. What's yours?"

"Barry. Nice to meet you."

"Did you enjoy your time in Hawaii?" I ask.

"Yes. It's very beautiful here," Barry says.

Barry has an English accent. Myles brings Barry his drink, and he smiles. My phone rings; it's Tony. I excuse myself from the bar to take the call.

"Hello."

"Hi, it's Tony. It's bright and early here in Tuscany, and I am working in the tasting room today."

"Hi. I'm leaving tomorrow and very much looking forward to going home, except you won't be there. I miss you," I reply.

"I have three months behind me and three months to go. I've loved every minute of it," Tony explains.

"I'm so glad you accepted Uncle Luca's offer," I smile.

"I am, too. I have to go, so we'll talk tomorrow. Have a safe trip home. I love you," Tony says and hangs up.

I walk back to the bar and am glad to see my barstool is still empty. I sit down next to Barry. He smiles at me and says, "Is everything OK?"

"Oh, yes, thanks for asking. I was talking to my boyfriend, who is in Tuscany, Italy, right now for six months. He is working on a vineyard and winery called CalaLuca. I'm very excited for him," I explain.

"That is very exciting," Barry says.

I wave to Myles and ask for a Mai Tai to go and the check. I have to leave pretty early tomorrow. Myles brings the drink and the check to the bar.

"It was nice meeting you, Barry. I love your accent," I smile.

"Nice meeting you, too," Barry says.

25

FLIGHT 642 IS now boarding at gate four. I made it from the hotel to the cab to the airport, through security, and to the gate. I board the plane, find my window seat, and crawl in for the long flight. *I didn't even bump my head while trying to sit down.* I look out the window and wonder how odd working here would be. I see the luggage carts and the food and drink expandable trucks.

"Excuse me."

I look away from the window and see a gentleman trying to sit next to me. I had my bag on his seat, but I move it to the floor and apologize.

He smiles and sits down. "Lolly, is that you?" He asks. "Do you remember me from the pool bar?" Barry says.

"Of course I do, and we are sitting next to each other on the flight home! What are the chances of that happening?" I reply.

I look back out the window while Barry gets situated. After the plane is boarded, the plane takes off, and the beverage service begins. I order a red wine, and Barry orders a white wine.

"So, where do you live since you're on my plane?"

"I live in Walnut Creek., Barry says. "Where do you live?

"I live in East Marin," I respond.

"So, why did you go to Hawaii?" Barry asks.

"It's a long story. I was a project manager in San Francisco for H&S Construction. I was laid off on Friday, the thirteenth, and I was devastated. I decided to go to Hawaii. I needed to regain my self-esteem and figure out what to do next."

"You work for H&S?" Barry asks.

'Well, I used to work for H&S," I explain. "What do you do?"

"I'm the president of Beevis, Inc. We are an international construction management company out of London. We are currently working with H&S on a high-rise in San Fransisco," Barry explains.

"So, you must know some of the guys I worked with," I say.

"As a matter of fact, I got a call a few weeks ago from Jose Animar, saying I may get a call from Loretta Novak, a project manager who was let go and might be looking for a job. Is that you?" Barry asks.

I move forward in my chair, face him, and scream lowly, "Yes, I'm Loretta Novak!"

Barry smiles at me. The drinks are delivered, and both of us are eager for a sip of wine in light of our recent discovery.

"It's a small world," Barry says. "In fact, I find it hard to believe that not only did I meet you at the pool bar at the hotel, but we are also seated next to each other on the plane home. Plus, I'm interested in hiring you and want to interview you for a position at my firm."

"I would like to interview for a position at your firm," I smile.

"Well, let's do it right here. I think the interview will be me telling you more about Beevis. You must understand who the company is and what it does. Even more important is me telling you about the position that I would be hiring you for," Barry continues.

"OK," I say. The stewardess brings new glasses of wine for us and a snack. We relax for a minute and settle in. We still have a few more hours on our flight.

About twenty minutes later, Barry turns to me and says, "I've been thinking. No interview is necessary. I would like to offer you a job as a project manager on the OMUD project. The project is for their headquarters in downtown Oakland. It is already staffed with a project executive, one project manager, and an administrator and is coming out of the ground with structural steel. Beevis has construction trailers on-site next to the contractor building the job, West Construction. The job schedule is eighteen months to complete. After that, the interiors would be bid out and built. Is this something you'd be interested in?" Barry asks.

"Do I have to accept the job right now?"

"Oh no, we're on a plane, for Christ's sake."

"Well, that's good, but the project does sound like something I'd be interested in. Thank you so much for giving me this opportunity."

"You're welcome, Lolly. I'll tell you what. In about a week, call me, and we can arrange for your first day and that kind of stuff. For now, let's relax and think about Hawaii for the next couple of hours," Barry smiles.

I stare out the window, looking over the Pacific, thinking how crazy my trip has been. To think I got a job offer in Row 24D—go figure. This is perfect. I already have a job when I land—no job searching, no interviews, no stress.

26

I DRIVE HOME from the airport at 3:00 p.m. on Monday. When I get to East Marin, I don't know if T and Cal are around. The yacht club is closed, so I stop by T's, and Cal is there.

"Hey," I say.

"Hi, Lolly."

"I just got back from Hawaii and didn't want to go home to an empty house yet," I exclaim.

"You can hang out here with me. Trisha should be home any minute now, depending on traffic," Cal says.

I sit next to the window, looking at the view of the City and bridges. "Can I get you a glass of wine?" Cal asks.

"Yes, please," I smile. "How is the living arrangement going?" I ask.

Cal brings me a big glass of red, sits down, and says, "We are doing great. I am so happy you introduced us. Trisha is a fun girl to be around. I love spending my time with her," Cal elaborates.

Just then, T walks through the front door. "Aloha," T says.

I get up and hug her. I missed my friends for a week, traveling alone. "Come sit with me. I have lots to tell you." T walks over and hugs Cal, thanking him for taking care of me while she wasn't there. T grabs a glass of wine, walks to the window, and sits. "So, did your 'Aloha Alone-a' work for you?" T asks, chuckling.

"I think so. I don't think I'd ever go on vacation alone again; hopefully, I'll never have a reason to. However, everything worked out—no travel issues. I made it to the Lahaina Yacht Club, which was special. The people I talked to most were mostly bartenders or patrons at the pool bar. I had some small talk with a fellow with a British accent last night. We ended up sitting next to each other on the plane, too. So, we got to talking, and he is the president of a construction management firm and offered me a job, sitting on the plane!"

"WHAT" T screams. "How could that happen?"

"It did. He gave me his card and said to call him in a week or so, and we can figure out when I want to start work," I smile. "I haven't even told Tony yet."

"How is Tony doing, anyway?" T asks.

"He's great. He has been there for three months, and he loves it. I'm so glad it's working out for him," I say. "I better get going. I haven't been home yet, but it's not like I have to go to work tomorrow."

I settle in at home, unpack, and realize I have to call Tony at 7:00 p.m., which is 7:00 a.m. Tuscany time. I pour a glass of wine and head for the balcony to sit and watch the bay. What a fabulous view, even compared to the ocean view off my hotel balcony. A little after 7:00 p.m., I call Tony. "Hello."

"Hi, this is Lolly. Are you awake?"

"Lolly," Tony says. "You're home. How are you?"

"I'm good. I have some great news. I met a guy at the hotel pool bar last night, and if you can believe it, he also sat next to me on the plane. We get to talking, and he's the president of a construction management firm called Beevis International. To make a long story short, he offered me a project manager position on a job in downtown Oakland," I explain.

"Wow, that's fantastic. It sounds like a great job for a great company," Tony says. "Are you sure he was serious?"

"It wasn't like he was drunk or anything. I just figured I'd call him next week. What have you been working on?" I ask.

"Do you remember when Uncle Luca was there, and we went to a winery called Ramey?" Tony asks.

"Yes."

"David Ramey visited CalaLuca Winery in Tuscany and asked Luca if he wanted to buy his winery. He is considering retiring but doesn't want to just list the property for sale. He wants to sell it to the right people."

"So, what did Uncle Luca say?" I ask.

"He said I would love to purchase your winery and vineyard, but I would have to staff the facility with my family."

"So, what does that mean?" I ask.

"I would come home and start working at Ramey Winery, but they will change the name to CalaLuca Winery."

"Is this what you want to do?" I ask.

"Absolutely. This is such a fabulous industry to be involved in. You, too, could be involved," Tony says. "And I might be home earlier than planned if I have to start at Ramey. We still have to talk about that. I'll call you later." Tony hangs up.

27

I CALL BARRY to tell him I'm ready to start work. He says, "Next Monday will work for Beevis International. Come to my office at 9:00 a.m. I'm on the eleventh floor at 1100 Broadway in downtown Oakland. Dress for the job site. I will take you there and introduce you to the staff you'll be working with. Maybe we can get a tour of the job site together."

I spent the rest of the week organizing a few things and shopping for work boots, jeans, and job site attire. Finally, it's Friday night, and I head to the yacht club to check in with Charles. I go early, so I have time to discuss my trip. I pull into the parking lot, run up the steps, and go in the back way. Only two others were in the bar, and I heard, "Lolly, you're home. Welcome back!"

This is the kind of homecoming I have been waiting for all week long. I sit at my usual bar stool, and Charles already has my usual wine in front of me. "Thanks," I smile.

"So, how was it? Did you make it to Lahaina Yacht Club?" Charles asks.

"Yes, I did—twice. As most yacht club bartenders do, Zak took care of me. He realized I was by myself and made sure I was having a good time. Between Zak and Myles, the bartender at the poolside bar at the hotel, I was well taken care of. You didn't call them and tell them I was coming, did you?" I ask Charles. "That's how special they treated me."

"I'm good but not that good," Charles smiles.

A few more members stroll in and walk up to the bar. I just stare out the window at the City, boats, and bridges while he does his job. He is working. I think it's social hour with me. Charles moves back to my spot with another glass of wine.

"Thanks. Just one last thing I have to tell you. I talked with a fellow with a British accent at the poolside bar the last night in Hawaii. It ended up he was seated next to me on the plane home and offered me a job at a job site in downtown Oakland. I start Monday," I explain.

"Good for you. See, I told you you'd be back!" Charles smiles.

Monday morning came quickly. Driving to Oakland is a different commute than driving to San Francisco; it's much easier from East Marin. I may be able to get used to this. I park in a parking garage and find my way to 1100 Broadway. I walk into the lobby and push the eleventh floor on the elevator. I walk out of the elevator on the eleventh floor and into the Beevis Incorporated offices. The receptionist greets me and says, "Welcome. What can I do for you?"

"My name is Loretta Novak, and I'm here to see Barry Bailey."

"Take a seat, and we'll be right with you," the receptionist says.

I take a seat, and a few moments go by. I look up and see Barry. "Lolly, so good to see you. Welcome to Beevis International. Come into my office so we can talk about your employment details."

I follow Barry to his office. We talk about salary, benefits, vacation, and the job description. I gather what they need is someone to review claims from the contractor. We leave the office at 1100 Broadway and walk to the job site four blocks down. Barry walks into the trailer. "Hi, Betty. How are you today? I'd like to introduce you to Loretta Novak. She is going to be working here." At that point, two guys rush out of their offices after hearing Barry introduce me.

"Well, now that both of you are here, I'd like to introduce Loretta Novak, our new project manager. Loretta, this is Phil Baker, senior project manager, and Fred Thompson, the project manager on this project."

"Welcome," Phil says. "We have a desk set up for you."

"Thank you," I say.

"Can we go take a quick tour of the construction site?" Barry asks. "This will get Loretta more familiar with where we are at with the construction schedule. She will mainly be dealing with the claims from the contractor."

The tour begins and ends, and I settle at my new desk. Fred and I are in a large room with a plan table. I realize my car is parked in a parking garage a few blocks up the street. "Can I park here tomorrow?" I ask.

Phil says, "Absolutely, it will take a couple of days for you to get organized and familiar with what to do."

"Barry, can I walk back with you to get my car from the garage?" I ask. "I don't want to walk through downtown Oakland by myself."

"Sure, I'm leaving right now, so gather your things. Tomorrow is a new day. Let's go," Barry says.

On the walk up the block, Barry asks if I fancy a drink. It is happy hour. I agree, and we stroll into an English pub called McGinnis. Barry orders a beer, and I order a wine.

"Welcome to Beevis. So, what do you think so far?" He asks. "It's only your first day, but you must have an opinion."

"Everyone on site seems pleasant, and the job is interesting. I just don't know about working in downtown Oakland. I'm used to San Francisco, and you'd think they were 10,000 miles away from each other—not twenty miles. It's hard to believe that culture can't cross the Bay Bridge," I explain.

He looks at me and says, "I agree with you, but in construction, you go where the work is. Most of Beevis' work is in Oakland. The good news is it's a fifteen-minute drive to San Francisco."

I drive to East Marin from Oakland, which is twenty minutes, swing into my driveway, walk up to the view, and smile. This place is very nice. A glass of wine and a seat on the balcony beats most places around here. I'll call Tony at 7:00 p.m. He should be up by then.

"Hello, this is Tony."

"Hi, it's Lolly. How are you?"

"I'm fine. How was your first day at work?" Tony asks.

"It was fine. I'll settle into the job site office tomorrow and maybe even do some work," I say. "What's new with CalaLuca Winery?" I ask.

"We're trying to come up with a day to close on the property, which would determine my return to the Bay Area."

"Have you kept your mom and dad up to speed about what's going on?" I ask. "I want to go to happy hour at Bertelli's this week. I miss them."

"That's nice, Lolly. They'd love to see you. They don't know anything about what Uncle Luca is doing. I talk to them every week, but this might be a little buffer for them to talk to you and not worry about me," Tony explains.

"OK. I won't say a thing. I can't wait to see you. I miss you so much. We'll talk tomorrow, bye," I say.

I drive to downtown Oakland the next day and park my Miata out of harm's way on the job site. I say good morning to everyone and take a seat at my desk. There is a large stack of papers on my desk, the claims from the contractor. It will take me a few days to get up to speed on the job.

My phone rings. I pick it up, and Betty says, "You have a call. It's Sadie Goldwater." Since I don't know anyone by that name, my first reaction was to decline the call, but I didn't feel comfortable doing that. "I'll take the call, Betty."

The phone on my desk rings, and I pick it up. "Hi, this is Loretta. Can I help you?"

"Hi, Loretta. This is Sadie Goldwater. How are you today?"

"I'm fine. Who are you?" I ask.

"How do you like working for Beevis International?" Sadie asks.

"How do you know that I work here? I don't even know you."

"I am a professional recruiter, and the reason I reached out to you is because I want to know if you know anyone who would be interested in a job as a project manager for a general contractor in downtown Oakland," Sadie explains.

"No, I don't." I hang up the phone.

28

I START WORK on my claims. Betty makes the best coffee in the world. I grab a cup and sit down to my stack of claims. I'm not too sure about this. About an hour passes, and Betty rings in. "You have a call from Sadie Goldwater."

"I'll take it," I say.

"Hi, this is Loretta."

"Good morning, this is Sadie. How are you today?"

"Busy, and I don't have time to talk right now," I say.

"I understand that, but you need to realize that I need you to help me do my job," Sadie says. "I make a lot of money—lots more than the positions I am trying to fill."

"I'm not interested in helping you," I say. "It seems like you make a lot of money without my help." I hung up the phone again.

Tomorrow is the first meeting with the contractor and the lawyer to discuss their claims. I have reviewed all the claims submitted by Stevenson Construction and responded positively or negatively. I'm ready for tomorrow's meeting. I confirm the meeting is here in the trailer at 10:00 a.m.

The next day, I arrived at the job site earlier than usual. Betty already has the box of donuts on the table and two pots of coffee brewing. "Thanks, Betty," I smile. "I guess this is an important meeting, especially for me."

"Don't worry, girl. You'll do fine," Betty says.

I start transporting all the documents from my desk into the conference room and pick a seat for me to operate from. I don't know how many people will be here, but we have room for twelve.

At 9:45, the trailer door opens, and Bob Clemson from Stevenson Construction walks in.

"Hi, I'm Loretta Novak. I'm reviewing your claim for Beevis."

"Hi, I'm Bob Clemson."

"Take a seat and grab a cup of coffee and a donut."

"Thanks," Bob says.

Minutes later, two other gentlemen I've never met come in. "Hi, I'm Loretta Novak, the project manager working on the claims."

He reaches out his hand to shake mine and says, "Hi, I'm Mark Mitchell, legal counsel for OMUD." I shake his hand.

"And I'm Gerry Black, OMUD construction manager for this project."

"Welcome. Everyone, take a seat and feel free to get a coffee and a donut. Who is running this meeting?" I ask.

The response is silence. Finally, Gerry speaks up, saying, "I think Mark Mitchell should facilitate the process."

"I wasn't prepared for this, but I can do it if you'd like, Gerry."

I cannot believe how disorganized it is, but I try to be as professional as possible, contributing to the meeting when possible.

Mark starts off by saying, "We're here to resolve several claims that Stevenson Construction has submitted for review. Beevis has reviewed them, and hopefully, we can come to a full resolution at this meeting. Let's get started."

"Loretta, why don't you start with your pile," Mark suggests.

"Fine. The first claim is for $247,900. It is for unforeseen conditions during excavation. My review of the costs submitted is approved," I say.

Gerry says, "Loretta, how do you know anything about construction?"

"I have a degree in civil engineering and job site and estimating experience," I explain.

"Well, I don't agree with your review of our first claim. What does Mark have to say about it?" Gerry asks.

Mark is startled by the request and admits he has to rely on the expertise of the construction manager reviewing the details. This is going to be a very long meeting if Gerry is going to challenge everything the rest of us come up with. The meeting breaks up four hours later, and there is a positive resolution for most things.

I head back to my desk with all my paperwork. Phil walks over and says, "How'd it go?"

"Well, I think Bob Clemson from Stevenson Construction and I were the only ones who knew anything about the issues at hand, but Gerry wanted to put his opinion into everything," I explain. "He said he wanted to meet with Beevis next week. I told him you'd call him."

I drove home and stopped at T's. She just got home, and Cal was out with a few buds.

"So, how is the new job going?" T asks.

"It's OK, but I don't feel the same way I did about H&S. It's weird. I was in a four-hour meeting today with a lawyer and the GC. The lawyer didn't know anything about the job. I bet he was making $450 an hour, sitting in this meeting, hardly contributing, and I knew every detail of every claim and probably made a quarter of what he makes.

"Enough shop talk. How's Cal doing?"
I ask.

"He's doing great. He loves living in East Marin. He loves me. What more can I ask for?" T says. "What's the latest with Tony?"

"He's into his fourth month and loving every minute. He shared some great news with me last week, but I'm not at liberty to say. You and Cal will be the first to know when it's official."

"That sounds exciting," T says.

The next evening, I head over to Bertelli's for happy hour. I left work a little early so I could make it. As I walk in the door, Maria runs to me and greets me with a big hug. "Lolly, you're here. We've missed you. We're lonely without Antonio and you visiting all the time."

"That's why I wanted to visit—to check out the infamous happy hour and visit with my favorite restaurant owners," I smile.

"Come sit over here at Tony's favorite table. I'll get some wine and food and tell Vinnie you are here," Maria says, very excited to see me.

"Thanks, Maria," I say.

A few minutes later, I look up and see Vinnie heading my way. I stand up, anticipating a Vinnie hug, which I've missed since Tony left. "How's my favorite Lolly?" Vinnie smiles.

"I'm fine. I miss Tony and Maria and you. That's why I came to visit. I think Tony is on the home stretch with his orientation—only a couple of months to go. I talk to him a lot," I explain.

"Well, sit down, and let's get you something to eat and drink. Where are our manners?" Vinnie wonders and he disappears into the kitchen.

I forgot how nice it is to come here. The next thing I know, a wine bottle, three glasses, and a plate of calamari show up. I smile. I never have to order here. Maria sits down and pours the wine. "So, tell me how my Antonio is doing. You probably talk to him more than we do, although he is very good at calling, even with the time difference," Maria says.

"He loves being in Tuscany. He loves everything he's learning about the business but misses home. However, he's hanging in there; only two more months to go, give or take a few days," I say.

"I'm glad to hear that from you. I figured he just might be sugarcoating his messages to us, but he wouldn't do that to you. He'd tell you what he really felt," Maria shares.

The next thing we know, Vinnie is bringing plates of food for all. I love this place.

29

I SHOW UP for work and don't know what to prepare for our 10:30 meeting. Phil hasn't given me any clue indicating what the meeting is about. Betty intercoms in and says Sadie is on line two. I pick up the line, "This is Loretta. Can I help you?"

"Hi. Sadie here, just checking in with you. I have no applicants for my downtown Oakland position."

"Have you ever been to downtown Oakland?" I ask.

"Oh, God no," Sadie says.

"I think you'd have a better understanding if you visited the towns you are trying to sell positions in," I state.

"No, I rely on my clients to fill in the applicants on the job environment," Sadie says.

"But isn't that after they agree to the interview?" I ask.

I look at the time. "I have to go. I have a meeting," I say and hang up.

Phil walks over and asks, "Are you ready for the meeting?" I don't know what to prepare for, so the answer is yes. I follow Phil into the conference room in the trailer, pour a cup of coffee, and sit down. Gerry Black enters the trailer and the conference room a few moments later. He closes the door behind him, gets a coffee, and sits down. Gerry looks at me and then at Phil. He begins by saying that he is not pleased with how I analyzed the claims. "I think there could have been much more rejection of the claims than acceptance," Gerry explains.

"But I..." Gerry cuts off Loretta and says, "Do not speak until spoken to. Did anyone else at Beevis International review Loretta's review?"

"She's a professional. That's why we hired her," Phil says.

"Well, I don't agree," Gerry states.

I look down at my lap, trying to understand what is going on. I'm not happy right now. I feel like getting up and walking out of the meeting, but I think I need to respect Beevis a little more and screw Gerry Black. I quietly turned my attention to the meeting without saying a word, as instructed.

"So, Gerry, what would you like Beevis to do at this point?" Phil asks.

"I would like you to review Loretta's work before we go to the negotiating meeting," Gerry says.

"We can do that, but the additional review of each claim will be charged to OMUD," Phil states.

"Oh, no. According to your original contract, Beevis needs to provide a review of claims with no additional cost to OMUD," Gerry explains.

"That's what Loretta is doing now, and it meets our contractual obligation. If this doesn't meet your standards, it is an additional cost to OMUD," Phil explains.

"I'll take this up with Barry. Have a nice afternoon." Gerry says as he walks out of the trailer.

Phil looks over at me and asks, "Are you OK?"

"No, I just need some time to digest all this bullshit. Pardon the French," I say.

"Let's go to McGinness and talk about it."

I return to my desk, pack my stuff, throw it in my car, and meet Phil for the two-block walk. "We should call Barry and ask him to join us," I exclaim. "I haven't seen him in weeks."

We arrive at the bar. Phil calls Barry, and he arrives in no time. "Is everything OK at the job site?" he asks.

"The job site is fine. It's just we had a meeting with Gerry Black today; he shared that he's not thrilled with Loretta's work. He wants us to review her work, and I told him we can do that—for an additional cost—which he refused. He said he'd take it up with you," Phil explains.

"How are you holding up, Lolly?" Barry asks.

"It was bullshit; I know that, maybe even politically driven. Beevis stood up for me, so thank you for that. I still need to think about some of the things he said that I didn't like," I say.

"I'm sorry you had to go through something like that with a client," Barry elaborates. "Let's order a round of drinks and talk about something else."

When the drinks arrive at the table, everyone cheers and sips. I still remember Gerry Black's comment: "Do not speak unless spoken to." That basically renders me completely useless, especially knowing my claims reviews are useless.

"Barry, are you sure you still want me to work here if the client won't accept my work?" I ask.

Barry looks at me, takes a swig of beer, and says, "Please don't take his remarks the wrong way."

"You mean there's a right way?" I ask. Barry and Phil laugh. "I don't know if you two can relate to what it's like to have a male chauvinist complain about your work. I know he's complaining because I'm female. Thanks to you two for not doing that. I'm going to have to take off. Thanks for the drink. See you tomorrow, Phil."

30

I SHOW UP for work again and realize I don't like what I'm doing here. I thought I was being very thorough and complete in my claims analysis. I want to be recognized for my work—not silenced. The job site phone rings. Betty picks up and says, "Line two, Loretta."

"Hi, this is Loretta."

"It's Sadie."

"I'm glad you called. A few things came up in the last few days, and I'm interested in the position you're selling," I explain. "Now, can you tell me about the company and the position?"

"I never, in a million years, would have thought you'd come to this. I'm not going to question it—just run with it. I apologize for not being more prepared, but I'm in shock. First, I need to set up an interview with Ron Palmer with 3C Construction. When are you available?"

"Tuesday or Thursday next week, 11:00 a.m. to 2:00 p.m.," I respond.

"OK. I'll see what I can do. Let me tell you a little about the position. From what I can tell, it doesn't require much skill. It's a project manager position in downtown Oakland," Sadie explains.

"So, I'd be working in Oakland again. That's unfortunate," I say. "You said before you've never been here. If you'd been here, you'd know what I'm talking about."

"How bad can it be?" Sadie asks.

"Well, the last time I walked up Broadway, which is the main drag through downtown, a drunk pulled his pants down and peed on a mailbox. I had to step out of his range. It was horrible," I tell her.

"Well, I think 3C Construction is at least ten blocks north of Beevis International," Sadie says.

"I don't know, but I think it's worse up there than downtown," I state.

"Let me get back to you on your interview time—if you are still interested," Sadie responds.

"I'm still interested. I just don't want to work on this project I am on right now," I say.

I head home and go straight to T's, hoping she's home. T answers the door and gives me a big hug. "You look like you can use this," T smiles.

"It's a long story. Wine is required," I say.

We make our way to a window seat with a view. T hurries to the kitchen to open a bottle of wine and grab two glasses. "Where's Cal?" I ask.

"He's in San Diego, visiting family," T says. "He gets back tomorrow."

T returns to the table with an open bottle and two glasses, pouring us both a nine-ounce pour.

"So, what is going on?" T asks.

"I've only been working at the job site for two months. All I do is review the contractors' claims. It's a public job, so there are lots of them. We had a big meeting last week with OMUD and a lawyer. I was completely prepared for all the reviews. Then, we had a separate meeting afterward, only to find that the client wanted my claim reviews reviewed. When I had a chance to speak my mind, I was told, 'Do not speak unless spoken to.'

"WHAT" T says.

"This guy is a dick, and I don't think I'm going to be able to work there much longer," I continue. "I can't work on a job site where the owner's rep doesn't respect my work."

"What are you going to do?" T asks.

"I don't know right now. This sleazy headhunter gal keeps calling me, so maybe I'll see what she has to offer. I have to go home and call Tony. I figured out there's a twelve-hour time difference, so if I call at 7:00 p.m. here, it's 7:00 a.m. there. It works out well," I explain.

I get up to leave. "We'll tell Tony hi for me."

"And tell Cal hi for me as well. I'll keep you posted," and I walk out the door.

I walk into the triplex, mail in hand. It's 6:45, so I have fifteen minutes to settle before I call Tony. I have an opened bottle of wine. I look in the fridge and have a few leftovers for dinner. I go downstairs to change into something more relaxing and return to pour a glass of wine and sit on the balcony. I called Tony.

"Hi, this is Tony."

"Hi, this is Lolly."

"How are you? I miss you," Tony says.

"I had some issues at work, and they will probably not go away. I've got it covered, though. I would much rather hear about how you are doing. I miss you so much," I say.

"Well, it's soon harvest, and I guess all hell breaks loose during harvest. I'll only be here for six more weeks, so I'm trying to learn as much as possible in every phase of the process," Tony says.

"I went to visit Bertelli's last week. I sat with your mom and dad at your favorite table and talked about you. It was great. They said they wanted to make sure you weren't sugar-coating your reports to them and wanted to hear from me, which I told them the truth about how happy you are over there. However, I didn't mention a thing about Uncle Luca buying property here," I say. "What's going on with that, anyway?" I ask.

"You are going to be happy about this. Right now, the plan is for me to leave here in two weeks and spend the last of the harvest and the crush in Sonoma at Ramey," Tony says.

"I get to see you in two weeks!" I say, smiling. "Where will you be?"

"I'll be in the thick of it at Ramey, but the closing of the property won't be done for a few weeks. I'll let you know when I'm coming home, and we'll talk soon," Tony says.

31

I CALLED SADIE to find out when my interview was scheduled. She tells me it's Thursday at 2:00 p.m. but can't talk now, so she'll call me back. I realize the general contractor, Stevenson Construction, is filing seventeen new claims. I sit back and realize how unmotivated I am to review any of these claims if OMUD doesn't respect my reviews and wants another review.

Betty rings in, "It's Sadie on line two."

I pick up. "Hi, Sadie."

"Hi, Loretta. Have you thought about your interview on Thursday at all?" Sadie asks.

"No. What do I have to think about? It's an interview. They ask questions; I answer questions, and it's over," I explain.

"There are many things you need to think about. First is your appearance. You must dress conservatively, maybe with a blazer over a blouse and a mid-length skirt. Your shoes should not exceed one inch in heel height. All the colors should be neutral, and all the materials should be non-transparent. This isn't the sexiest outfit you've ever worn," Sadie explains.

"I wanted to share with you that I know about this stuff. I am a professional and make $150,000 a year."

"That's probably more than you will be offered for this position, but I'm used to that. I want you to also be conservative on your make-up. No false eyelashes or red lipstick. Go for the natural look," Sadie reveals.

Who does this girl think she is—better than everyone else?

"And don't wear too much perfume. Your hair needs to be in control, not flying all over. So, what do you think?" Sadie asks.

"I think I have to go. I'll be there on Thursday. Thanks," I say and hang up the phone.

My blood pressure is rising. It's hard to believe that a headhunter—who has never met me and claims to be a professional—would feel the need to tell me what kind of shoes to wear and how much perfume to wear. My mind is racing, and I think I have a plan for Thursday's interview.

I told Phil I had a doctor's appointment and needed some time. I jump into the Miata and drive to a parking garage close to 3C's offices in Oakland. In the parking garage, I park in a relatively sparse area and start undressing. Work boots and pants came off first. Nylons, skirt, and shoes came next. My skirt was almost a mini skirt. It is white. My three-inch-heeled shoes are red. I put on a tight tee shirt for a top and head to the office for my interview.

I get to the offices of 3C Construction and walk into the lobby. "Hi, My name is Loretta Novak, and I have an interview with Ron Palmer."

"Take a seat, and I'll let Ron know you are here."

I look around the office at the construction pictures on the wall, and Ron walks out and heads straight for me. I stand up. "Loretta Novak?"

"Yes," and shake his hand.

"Come on back to my office, and we can talk," Ron says.

I walk into his office, sit on the chair across from his desk, and cross my legs. He sits down and stares at my legs. "Can I get you something to drink?"

"No, thank you."

"So, you work for Beevis on the OMUD project, and before that, you were with H&S, correct?" Ron states.

"Yes, I was with H&S for ten years until the work dried up, and they laid me off. That's how I ended up on the OMUD project as a claims reviewer," I share.

"Well, I know Barry Bailey and Hank Evans. Hank and I are good friends. I think we've met before, maybe at a job walk or a pre-bid meeting. I'm not sure," Ron explains.

"I think I met you at the tenant improvement job walk for Pacific Inc. at 1111 Broadway," I say.

"That's right. You were there with Hank, and he introduced me to you," Ron says.

I smile and say, "Is 3C going to bid on the OMUD tenant improvements in a few months?" I ask.

"Absolutely," Ron says. "It's a sweet job, around $12 million. I'm also interested in offering you a job, and if I play my cards right, you'll come to work for me. 3C will get the OMUD TI; you can be the project manager. How does that sound, Loretta?"

"That sounds good, but I'll have to think about it. You must know that your headhunter, Sadie, is quite a piece of work. She called a lot and told me what to do on my interview like I was straight out of college, but almost to the point of insulting me. I didn't care for that," I say.

"Her tactics work. She's gotten plenty of commissions from me and, hopefully, will get another one if you accept the position. Why don't you think about it, and we'll talk in a few days," Ron smiles.

"Thanks for your time, Ron." I stand up and walk out of the office. I get the Miata out of the parking garage and head straight for T's house. Her car is there, so I stop and knock on the door. Cal answers. "Hi, Lolly. You're home early and looking all dressed up. Come on in. T is already at the window with a glass of wine. Why don't you join her, and I will bring one for you."

"Thanks, Cal. It's good to see you," I say. I walk and sit down next to T. She says, "What's new? Last time we talked, you were telling me about the dick at OMUD," she says as Cal brings my wine.

"Well, I had an interview today at 3C Construction. They are in downtown Oakland, which I'm not too thrilled about. They offered me a position before I left the interview, but I don't think I would ever take the job if the headhunter, Sadie, gets a commission," I explain.

"So, now, what are you going to do?" T asks.

"Well, I do have some good news. Tony is coming home in less than two weeks, and his first assignment is harvest at Ramey Winery. The rest is even more exciting, but it's not a done deal yet, so I'll share the details as they happen. I'm just so excited he will be home soon," I smile.

"That's fantastic," T says. "Even Cal and I are ready for football parties and wine tasting when Tony returns."

"How are you two?"

"We're good. He's waiting for his next job. He's a bit nervous about it, but I'm working and hopefully able to hold out the lull," T explains.

"I'm glad things are working out for you two," I smile.

32

I CALL TONY the second I get home. He's just waking up, and I can tell he has something to tell me. I told him about the interview and said I would never accept it if that crazy headhunter would get a commission.

"So, what's going on? I'm so excited you will be home soon," I say.

"Well, I've been meeting with Uncle Luca all week, and guess what?" Tony asks.

"What?"

"Uncle Luca is giving the property to me and you. He loves you more than I do, and that's almost impossible since I love you more than life itself," Tony explains. "However, that means that you and I will have to work on the vineyards and tend to the winery and everything else to run the business."

I am speechless. I can't think of anything to say. "Lolly, are you still there?" Tony asks.

"Yes, I'm just overwhelmed with Uncle Luca's generosity and confidence in you—and me, for that matter—and that this is a good idea. How are you feeling about all this?" I ask.

"Well, I learned so much working in Italy. I feel like I'm ready to take this on, but the first thing I have to do when I get home is talk about you. I want you to come work at the winery full-time. You need to quit your job. You need to learn every aspect of the business. Next, we need to hire a few people to help, but that will come in time. The Ramey help will be there through harvest to help with the transition. I still need to understand how the Sonoma County winery business works regarding property ownership, marketing, and events," Tony says.

"When are you scheduled to come home?" I ask.

"Uncle Luca said to pack up and get back to Lolly and Sonoma County. He promised to come to visit the new venture soon. So, my flight is tomorrow. Can you pick me up at the airport the next day? I'll send you the itinerary," he asks.

"Absolutely. I may even quit my job tomorrow. It sounds like you have plans for me," I say.

"I have plenty of plans for you, sweetheart," Tony smiles. "I need to hang up. I'll see you in a few days."

I hang up, pour myself a glass of wine, and sit on the deck overlooking the bay. I just stare; I'm not fully believing what I just heard. What I think I heard is Tony and I are going to own a winery and vineyard property. I'm still not quite sure it's real, but with the moon on the bay tonight, I'm going to relax and let it all sink in.

I wake up and have a cup of coffee. I have to quit today. Barry will not be very happy, but I will still be friends with him. Before I resign, I must call Sadie. I drive to downtown Oakland for hopefully the last time and walk into the trailer. First is Sadie. She answers and says, "So, I assume you love Ron and 3C Construction, and you want to accept the position."

"You've got to be kidding me. Go fuck yourself, Sadie. You are the , most insulting person I have ever worked with. I would never accept a position that earned you a commission," and hang up.

Next, I have to tell Phil that I'm quitting as of today. The reason is the manager of OMUD's sexist behavior, but the real reason is that Tony and I have a winery to manage and property to maintain. I walk up to Phil's office and knock on the door. He looks up and says, "Come on in. Have a seat."

I walk in, sit down, and smile.

"What can I do for you?" Phil says.

"I am going to resign from my position here. You know that I wasn't very happy when OMUD wanted to review my work, but I couldn't take his rude remarks. I can't work like that," I explain.

"I understand, but Beevis can find another spot for you somewhere else," Phil says.

"Thank you for that, but I have a new opportunity to own vineyard property in Sonoma County and work at the winery full-time, and I'm going for it," I say.

"Wow," Phil says. "That sounds like an incredible opportunity. I think I'd do the same if I were you. We have to try to get a hold of Barry and have a drink to celebrate your departure. Let's call Barry right now." He phones Barry, and he answers. "Hi, Phil. What's going on?" Barry asks.

"Loretta has resigned, and I wondered if you fancy a drink after work?" Phil asks.

"What do you mean she resigned?" Barry asks.

"She quit to have a better future in the winery business and get out of the construction business," Phil says.

"I'll meet you at McGinnis in fifteen minutes," Barry says.

I pack up my desk and take my things out to the Miata. I guess I should be sad about leaving this job, but I'm not because OMUD management was so rude to me. I'm just glad to see Barry before I leave.

Phil and I arrive at McGinnis and see Barry sitting at a table. He stands, walks over to us, and hugs me. "I never would have thought you would be in this position to be resigning so soon," Barry says.

"You know that I was unhappy with the remarks from OMUD," I say. "Plus, I got an opportunity to own and operate a vineyard and winery in Sonoma County, and I'm going for it. However, I'm glad I met you in Hawaii and would like to stay friends."

"I would like that, too," Barry smiles.

33

I PULL INTO the yacht club. I have to tell Charles the news. I approach the bar. "Hi, Lolly. What can I get you?" Charles asks.

"Hi. Yes, please—a Zinfandel. I have lots to tell you when you get a minute."

He delivers my wine and tends to two other members. He pours himself a beer and comes right over.

"So, que pasa?" Charles asks.

"Well, I quit my job at Beevis. The manager for OMUD was a dick and didn't respect my work. He wanted someone at Beevis to review all my work for no extra cost, basically do it twice. Anyway, that's not the exciting part," I say.

"Tony comes home tomorrow, and the two of us now own and operate Ramey Winery and Vineyards in Sonoma County. I'm going to work there full-time. Can you believe it?" I ask.

"Wow, where did this all come from?" Charles asks.

"Well, Uncle Luca met David Ramey when he was here earlier this year. Then, Tony went to Tuscany to work and learn from Uncle Luca. David went to Tuscany and met Luca and Tony at their winery. David said he was retiring and asked if Luca and Tony would be interested in Ramey. Luca said absolutely. The rest is history," I say.

"Wow, again," Charles says. "I thought you worked in construction."

"I did, but this is so different. I can't wait to get started."

I pull up at the airport, and Tony is already standing there. I am so excited to see him after five months; I can barely speak. I park and get out of the car. I don't care if they tow the car. I am giving my man the welcome home he deserves. He is standing by his luggage, and I run toward him and kiss him as long and passionately as possible. He hangs onto me like he doesn't want to let go. I don't want him to let go, either. He comes up for air but plants another one on me, and we sway in the breeze for a few moments.

"Excuse me; is this your vehicle?" the airport security guard asks.

Tony continues to kiss me, standing right on the curb and ignoring the security guard.

"I said excuse me," the guard states.

"Can we just have a few minutes? We are not doing anything wrong, and we are doing everything right, so please, just a few minutes," Tony pleads.

The guard backs off and watches as Tony and I continue our welcome. I missed him and can hardly believe he is on US soil. Tony finally pulls back and says, "We've got to go. We can stop at my place. The renter moved out last week. Then, we can meet my parents for dinner at the restaurant."

We are stuck in miserable traffic from SFO through downtown, but once we're over the Golden Gate Bridge, it clears up. Tony stares at the bridge like he's never seen it before. It is beautiful.

We make it to his house. I open a bottle of wine while he unloads the trunk and brings everything into his bedroom. We meet in the middle, and I say, "We can have some fun now, or we can have some fun later. Your choice."

"I want to have fun now, but I want to see my parents. The sooner we go down there, the sooner we will be back. Let's go."

We jump in the car and head to the restaurant. I thought I was excited to see him; he is forty times more excited to see Vinnie and Maria. It's very cute when a man is delighted to see his parents. We pull into the parking lot and get out of the car. Tony comes around, opens the door, and helps me out. I kiss him again and say, "Let's celebrate."

We walk into the restaurant. There's a crowd inside. Tony makes a direct path to his favorite table, trying to find his parents. Vinnie and Maria are waiting for him to arrive but at a different table. He finally figured it out and damn near attacked his parents with love and hugs. Tony had never been this far away from his parents. He may not want to be this far from his parents ever again.

"Come take a seat, Lolly," Vinnie says.

I sit next to Vinnie on one side and Maria on the other.

"We are so excited to see Tony. Thank you for picking him up from the airport," Maria says.

"My pleasure," I say.

Tony takes a seat at the table with his mom and dad. "I have exciting news to tell you, but let's order some wine first, and you can tell me what's new here," Tony says.

"Well, business has been booming at both the restaurant and the deli," Maria shares. "The parking lot got repaved, and the outside of the restaurant painted." Tony starts to open a bottle of wine and pours everyone a glass.

"Cheers. Here's to a wonderful stay with Uncle Luca," Tony smiles. Everyone takes a sip.

"Lolly and I have some exciting news to tell you."

"You're getting married!" Maria screams.

"No, mom. It's something way better than that, although getting married would be nice," Tony says, looking into my eyes with his bright blues.

"Well, tell us already, and I can order some food for all of us," Vinnie says. Tony waits until Vinnie places the order to start. Everyone takes another sip of wine.

"So, I'd like to thank Uncle Luca for allowing me to live, learn, and work on his magnificent vineyard and winery. However, he also did something else for me that will change our lives. He purchased Ramey Vineyard and Winery in Healdsburg from David Ramey, whom we met when Uncle Luca was visiting earlier this year. He wants Lolly and I to live there and run the business," Tony explains.

"When is all of this going to happen?" Vinnie asks.

"Well, the first thing we have to do is visit the winery and have you both meet David. We can do that tomorrow if it works for you. The property won't close for a few weeks, but David wants Lolly and I to work the harvest and get adjusted to everything before he retires," Tony says.

"Maria, do you want to go to the winery tomorrow?" Vinnie asks.

"Yes, I can't wait. It will be like another part of our family business."

"I'm going to check on dinner. I'm starving," Tony says.

"Grab another bottle of wine while you are at it," I say.

Tony returns to the table with fried calamari, spaghetti, meatballs, pork chop Milanese, served family style, and a bottle of CalaLuca Sangiovese. He couldn't wait to eat. It had been five months since he ate any of Bertelli's dishes, which are always fabulous. I love them, too.

Once we finish dinner, Tony asks, "What time do you want us to pick you up tomorrow morning?"

"10:30," Maria says. "We can get a coffee or a latte here and head to Healdsburg."

"Perfect. Goodnight, Mom. Goodnight, Dad. It's nice to be home. See you tomorrow," Tony waves, and Lolly waves to Maria and Vinnie as well.

34

WE PULL INTO the driveway of Tony's house. He turns to kiss me before we get out of the car. We make it into the house, and I pour two glasses of wine while he goes to unpack. I just sit back in the living room, thinking about tomorrow. I'm very excited about seeing the winery. Everything will be new to us. I assume there's a place for us to live on the property. I also assume there will be many employees we will meet, hoping to offer them employment after the closing. Tony returns to the living room, wine glass in hand, and sits right next to me.

"I'm looking forward to going to the winery," I say.

"I am, too. After we meet David, we'll hopefully get a tour of the vineyard and the facilities. Mom and Dad might have to sit that part out. Maybe David can have a little snack for them while we get the tour. I'm assuming we'll start work there the following day to get involved with the harvest and jump right in," Tony explains.

"I think this will be very fun. You already learned the ropes in Tuscany, but I still have much to learn," I say.

"Come here, and why don't we quit the shoptalk until tomorrow and start having our own fun." Tony puts his arms around me and kisses me. I fall into his arms. It has been too long. There's no reason to wait any longer.

We both have smiles on our faces when we wake up. There's no need to get out of bed right this minute if we're not going to Bertelli's until 10:30. Laying by his side and listening to his heartbeat almost makes me fall back asleep. Tony may have dosed off, too. How nice is this?

We get to the restaurant at 10:15, enough time to sit and relax and get a latte, coffee, scone, or muffin. We head up the road at exactly 10:30. Tony remembers how to get there. This place is not on a main drag. It is back in the countryside, with grape vines surrounding the small winery building. We get out of the car, look around for a minute, and smell the fresh air. All you can see on the rolling hills are grape vines with grapes on them. We walk into the winery, a beautiful space with a ten-foot door, high ceilings, and lots of wood. We look around and see David Ramey sitting, waiting for us.
"Hi. Welcome to Ramey Winery." David says.
"Hi. I'm Tony Bertelli. You remember me from visiting CalaLuca in Tuscany," Tony says.
"Absolutely! You are going to help the next three weeks to make it through harvest," David grins.
"Yes, but let me introduce you to everyone with me today. This is my girlfriend, Lolly. She'll be staying here and working with us. This is my mom, Maria, and my dad, Vinnie. They have a restaurant in Larkspur called Bertelli's and an Italian deli in Larkspur Landing called Bertelli's Italian Deli," Tony explains.
"It's so nice to meet everyone," David says. "Uncle Luca told me about you two. I'm looking forward to going to your restaurant after I retire. So, let's head to the tasting bar and get going on some of the vintage wines we are pouring today. First, we have a Sangiovese for you to taste. Because of its ability to be a chameleon, this wine offers a wide range of tastes, from earthy to rustic, as is the case with many Chiantis.

The grapes are grown on our property. These are the grapes that will be harvested this week."

David pours each of us a sip and moves on to the next one. We all take a sip.

"Our next one is a Primativo, also grow on our property but fairly new to the property. It is an Italian red grape that produces bold wines with smooth flavors of blackberry, dark chocolate, and licorice. We planted it in 2006, and it has produced a fabulous vintage for the six last years."

We all taste this one. It's very good.

"Our third and final taste will be the Syrah. This vintage is bold and full bodied, with aromatic notes of smoke, black fruit, and pepper spice. It's grown in the Dry Creek Valley, about ten miles from here."

David pours us tastes, and we all take a sip.

"I think I like this one the best," Vinnie says.

"I like all of them," Maria smiles.

"Me, too," I say.

"I think we need to purchase a mixed case for the restaurant," Vinnie explains.

"Perfect," David says. "The next thing we have to do is tour the wine cellar, the facilities, and the vineyard. Vinnie, do you and Maria want to stay here while Tony and Lolly come with me? It should only take thirty minutes. The two of you can sit out on the covered deck and look at the view. I'll open a bottle of your choice," David says.

"We'll be fine here getting to know the place. We even brought some snacks from our Italian deli. We'll get those out of the car, and you guys can have some when you return," Maria explains.

"Thanks, David," Vinnie says.

"I'll have Robert get you two set up on the porch. He'll get you a bottle of your wine of choice and help set the snacks up. Tony and Lolly, come with me. I have an ATV out front. Use the restrooms, and I'll meet you there in five," David says.

Tony and I find the bathrooms, part of the learning curve. We sit in the ATV and wait for David.

"So, what do you think so far?" Tony asks.

"I love it. I think Vinnie and Maria love it, too, and they intend to spend much time here. Just like they said, this is just like one of our family properties. I know they are at the restaurant most of the time, but that may change, just like everything else in our lives," I explain.

Tony smiles and puts his arm around me. "This is going to be pretty wild." David comes out of the winery, jumps in the ATV, and looks at the two of us. "Are you ready?" he asks.

"Absolutely!" Tony and I say simultaneously.

We first head to the wine-making facility in the middle of the property.

"This is where we receive all the grapes, crush them, barrel them, age them, and bottle them. The next three weeks will be all about receiving and crushing, but we will get into that first thing tomorrow."

David takes the ATV to the farthest end of the vineyard. "This is where you two will live, temporarily. You can move in tomorrow if you'd like."

"Wow," I say.

We make our way to the other side of the property, through the grapevines, and come to a huge home on top of a hill. "This is where my family lives until we close on the property. We should be moved out by then, and you and Lolly can do what you please with the property. That's up to you. Maybe you want to make this the temporary place for Vinnie and Maria to stay," David says.

"They would love having their own place here!" I say to Tony.

"I agree," Tony says.

"Our only other spot on the tour is the office. It's connected to the tasting room. There are a few offices, a storage room, and a conference room. I'd love to talk to you about how we use that space another time. Let's head back to the patio and find Vinnie and Maria."

"Sounds good, David. Thanks for the tour. We can talk about details for tomorrow before we leave," Tony explains.

"Perfect. Let's park the ATV and go relax," David says.

We walk through the tasting room to the patio. Maria and Vinnie are sitting there, relaxing and looking around like they are on vacation, eating snacks and sipping Syrah.

"Hi, guys. We got a great tour of the property. It's a lot to digest in one afternoon, but for now, Lolly and I will join you for some Syrah and snacks," Tony says. "Is that OK?" Tony asks.

It almost looked like we were disturbing them. They look so relaxed, gazing at the view. The vineyards are beautiful. They finally say, "Come join us. Tell us what you saw."

Tony and I sit, pour ourselves wine, and enjoy the wonderful snacks from the deli.

"Well, we went to see the wine-making facility. I have a feeling I will be spending a lot of time there. Next, we saw our temporary housing for the next three weeks. Then, we saw the Ramey Family home, which they will be moving out of by the time the property closes, and last, we saw the offices for the business, which are connected to the tasting room. It was quite the tour but only scratched the surface. Lolly and I have an awful lot to learn about this place," Tony says.

"Who will move into the Ramey Family house after they leave?" Maria asks.

"Probably Lolly and me. However, we already thought it would be great if you and Vinnie could take over the smaller cottage as your place to visit and hang out with us when you want," Tony says.

"I would love that," Maria says. "I love it here. It will be nice to get away from Larkspur occasionally."

"That's why I told you this place will change our lives—all of them, for the future, for the better—because of the amazing gift Uncle Luca gave us. I promise that Lolly and I will work hard to ensure our family business is something the family will be proud of," Tony explains.

David returns to the table. "Did you get some deli snacks?" I ask.

"Yes, and I may need the address of that place, too," David smiles. "I'll have Robert bring out your mixed case of wine and send you all on your way. I will see you and Lolly tomorrow."

"What time and where should we meet you on the property?" Tony asks.

"8:00 a.m. at the wine facility. We have a lot to go over," David says.

"OK, let's go. Thank you, David, for the great tour and wine tasting. See you tomorrow."

35

WE DRIVE TO the restaurant and head straight for Tony's favorite table. I think we're all pretty exhausted and starving. Tony goes to the back to order for us and brings a Ramey Syrah for dinner.

"So, Lolly, are you going to move there?" Maria asks.

"Yes, eventually. It's a fabulous property. Now, it's just working out all the details. Right now, I will focus on what Ramey needs for harvest, and the next three weeks will only concentrate on harvest. Talk about a quick way to learn," I say.

Tony returns to the table and sits, looking at all of us. "Well, what do you think?"

"Uncle Luca knocked it out of the park with this one. He has a family tradition he wants us to continue with CalaLuca Winery in Sonoma County," Vinnie says. "I think we can do that."

"I think we can, too," Tony says. "The fact that we will own that property and all the houses and buildings is almost overwhelming. I thought owning the restaurant was big, but this is much bigger. It will take some time for it just to sink in."

"Will we keep the name the same or change it?" I ask.

"That's a great question," Tony says. "I see us changing the name to CalaLuca, but I don't know if David would agree. He also wants to continue a legacy, so we'll have to play it by ear."

Finally, wine is poured, and dinner is served. We all had a long, amazing day at our new winery. Dinner is fabulous, as usual. Tony stands, walks over to me, and says, "We have to go back there tomorrow morning and get our first day of instruction from David. It might be a long three weeks, but it might be the greatest three weeks of our lives. We will see. Goodnight."

We walk out to our car and head to Tony's house. We arrive, and I have so many questions. Are we supposed to move and stay there tomorrow or drive back home? What am I supposed to do with my triplex? I walk into his house and grab Tony, putting my arms around him.

"You're amazing. This may be the most amazing thing that has ever happened to us—to me. Thank you for including me in the family tradition," I say.

"Come here. I think you know that this is a big step forward for us, and maybe I assumed you'd be up for it. We never really talked about it, and now that it's happening, we need to just do it," Tony says.

"I know. I know, and we really have to manage what we got ourselves into and enjoy the process," I say.

"We will do just that," Tony smiles and pulls me into a kiss that reflects everything that happened today.

We arrive at Ramey at 7:45 the next day with suitcases in our hands, but first, we go to the wine-making facility. We'll unpack at our cottage later. David drives up in the ATV. We exchange good mornings and wait to hear David's instructions.

"Good morning," David says. "The grapes are scheduled to be delivered in about half an hour. You two need to log the number of tubs as they come in and mark the weight of the grapes. Here is a spreadsheet for you to document that information. This way, the winemaker can concentrate only on the harvest. You will be gathering information for him."

"Aren't you the winemaker?" Tony asks David.

"No, not anymore. I hired a fellow named Adam from the UK a few years back. He's worked out very well."

"Thanks, David," Tony says.

In a few minutes, a truck carrying the grapes arrives. They pull on the scale. We register the weight. He tells me to get the bin number and write it on the same spreadsheet. I think that this will be the process all day long. After a couple of hours, we figured it out.

David shows up out of nowhere to check on us.

"You guys doing OK?" David asks.

"Yeah, we're fine. Can we have lunch now?" Tony asks.

"You two can come with me, and we'll have lunch on the patio," David says.

We jump into the ATV and say, "Thanks, David."

The ATV drives all the way to the patio and lets everyone off. We walk onto the patio and are not sure what to do next. Dave returns, pointing to the spot where we will be eating. The patio is crowded, and I wonder if it's this crowded all the time.

We make our way to the table. We order a glass of wine and request menus. I don't know if David plans to have lunch with us.

The wine and menus come, and we eat lunch. Then, we head back to the grapes. We have work to do. We clock twenty-five more deliveries of grapes before we are ready to call it quits. Tony is ready to settle in the small cottage for the night. I am, too.

We return to our car and somehow find the cottage on the property. Tony removes the suitcase from the truck and heads to the front door. Tony puts the key in the door, and we walk into our new, temporary home. Both of us look around; it's nice and open, with a little living room and kitchen, a small table, and a bedroom and bathroom off the back.

"So, what do you think?" Tony asks.

"I think it's great. It's only temporary, and this is day one. We might need to go to the grocery store tomorrow to buy lunch and dinner stuff," I say.

"For now, let's just relax, kick back, and enjoy being here. I'll take the suitcase to the bedroom and pour us glasses of wine. We can talk about the next couple of days," Tony explains.

I look for a blanket in the closet and snuggle on the couch. Tony comes with the wine and sits next to me.

"My mind is racing. There is so much to digest. I need to meet the winemaker in the next day or so."

"And I need to meet the rest of the staff from the tasting room, the restaurant, and accounting. Maybe David will help do that soon. I can do what we did today by myself, and you can go off with David and see what's next on the agenda for harvest," I say.

"Actually, that might work. I should get David to layout the harvest plan over the next three weeks and talk more specifically about some of the tasks that he needs to be done so we can be as productive as possible," Tony defines. "We need to go home in a few days to see Maria and Vinnie, have dinner at Bertelli's, and pack more clothes."

"What about dinner for tonight?" I ask.

"Do you think there is a pizza place that delivers around here?" Tony laughs.

36

OUR FIRST NIGHT at the winery wasn't anything special, but it was very special to us. Our first night on this property—our property—will go down in history as a CalaLuca and Bertelli tradition. We don't even have any coffee to make, so we shower, dress, and drive to see if there is coffee anywhere. In the tasting room, there is a carafe of coffee for the staff, so we help ourselves and then head up the hill to find David and the grapes. David is sitting in the ATV, talking on his phone about the schedule of today's grapes.

"Good morning, you two. How was the cottage?" David asks.

"Perfect. We just need a few groceries, and we'll be set," Tony says. "Lolly and I talked about her taking over the grape inventory task and me going off with you to meet the winemaker and understand a better overall three-week harvest plan so we can be as productive as possible for you," Tony defines.

"Well, that's funny because I devised the same plan for today. Lolly can run to the grocery store later this afternoon because the grape deliveries should begin in about thirty minutes and be done by 2:00 p.m.," David says.

"OK, perfect. Let's go," Tony says.

The ATV drives away, and I sit and stare, looking out over the property. The more this sinks in, the more numb I get. It is hard to believe that Tony and I are responsible for this entire vineyard, including the harvest. I see the first truck pull up to the scale. These are the Sangiovese grapes from this property that are being harvested. I log the weight and the bin number, and the day begins.

Tony and David start their day at the wine-making facility. They walk in and see the crushers. Adam walks over. "Hi, Adam. This is Tony Bertelli. He is the new owner of the winery," David says.

"Hi, Tony, glad to meet you," and they shake hands.

"So, what is your most important task today?" David asks.

"Get the first crush of the Sangiovese to the fermentation tanks. I think that will become a routine," Adam says.

"And what do you need Tony to help you with?"

"If he looks over the crushers while I make sure the tanks are ready, I think it could run very smoothly."

"Tony, are you familiar with the crushing equipment?" David asks.

"Yes," Tony says.

"Well, that's solved. I'll be back in a few hours to see how things are going," David says.

I fill all my spreadsheets with tag numbers and weights, and the trucks stop coming. I finish, head back to the cottage, freshen up, and head to a grocery store. I have a list of what we need for the next three weeks. Once all the groceries are in the cottage, Tony arrives, walks up to me, and kisses me. I smile at him.

"How are you?"

"I'm fine. I'm making you chicken alfredo tonight. Is that OK?" I ask.

"It sounds great."

"How was your day with Adam?"

"You know all the grapes that came in yesterday, we crushed them today," Tony says. "We will do the same thing tomorrow if that's OK with you."

"I don't know if the grapes are still arriving tomorrow. I'm sure David will let us know. If not, I would like to check out the tasting room—who works there, the business practices, their hours, etc."

"That sounds great," Tony smiles.

"We also have coffee for tomorrow morning and lunch for the next few days, so we don't have to worry about that. We do have to pick a time when we can drive back down to Larkspur and hit East Marin, your apartment, and the restaurant," I explain.

Dinner is served.

The next morning, I go to the scales. David shows up and says, "Today should be the last day for Sangiovese. The Primitivo grapes won't start arriving until next week. Lolly, if you want, we can talk about the tasting room, our vendors, and our staff tomorrow to familiarize you with our business."

"I'd like that."

Tons of grapes arrive. Tony and Adam are still crushing. I see what they mean when they say harvest is intense. There is a very small window of time to do many things, but the Sangiovese wraps up its harvest today. I went home early and started a notebook for tomorrow. I told David I'd meet him in the office at 8:00 a.m. I even have enough time to cook dinner. Tonight, we'll have stuffed pork chops.

I arrive at the office at 8:00 a.m., and David is waiting for me. I grab a cup of coffee and meet him in the conference room. I wander over to the map of the property on the wall. I love maps.

"Good morning, Lolly. Since the map has caught your fancy, let's start with that. As you can see, the forty-nine-acre property has been color-coded by grape varietal and vineyard function. The vineyards for Primitivo are yellow; Sangiovese are pink; the residences are green; public facilities are blue, and offices and wine-making facilities are purple," David explains.

"Has Tony seen this yet?" I ask.

"I don't think so. I will arrange for that to happen," David says.

"It just is the big picture. I love it," Lolly smiles.

"So, let's move on to the tasting room. The hours of operation are 11:00 a.m. to 4:00 p.m. We charge a tasting fee of $10.00. That fee is waived if they buy one bottle of wine. You'd be surprised to know how many bottles we sell just because they get to save the tasting fee. It's funny. We have two full-time employees. Robert manages the tasting room and provides tasting to the customers, and Mary handles the accounting, website, marketing, and special events. Hopefully, you will meet Mary shortly," David continues.

"You do a lot of pouring yourself. I might have to fill that spot, but of course, you'd be hard shoes to fill," Lolly smiles. "Who is responsible for the actual wine sales?" I ask.

"That's a great transition to the vendor part of our meeting. We are using a company called Sonoma Distributing to sell our wines to retail, restaurants, bars, and other points of sale," David explains.

"The tasting room is also responsible for direct sales, right?" I ask.

"Yes. Robert and Mary have the retail side of the tasting room figured out," David states. "Let's move on to the restaurant. We have a month-to-month lease with Southerly's to provide food and staff to the winery," David says.

"What are the terms of their lease?" I ask.

"Thirty days' notice to vacate. It's a pretty slim operation, so it couldn't take much more than that to get out," David explains.

"Do you need a license to grow and sell wine in California?" I ask.

"Absolutely," David says. "Ramey has everything you need. You need to write down in your notebook to transfer the license as soon as escrow closes."

"What else does the City of Healdsburg or Sonoma County require—inspections, taxes, etc?" I ask.

"I have a tax advisor, Ralph, for all that kind of stuff. I'll introduce you and Tony to him before I'm out of here," David says. "What other questions do you have?"

"Do you have a website?" I ask.

"Yes, it's **rameywinery.com**," David says.

"Do you host many private events?" I ask.

"Not many. There is a big barn on the property that we used to host a wedding, but it was very small. We don't advertise for the barn," David explains.

"OK. I just wanted to know. Who maintains the property?" I ask. "Landscaping, irrigation, the vineyards."

"Our long-time family of Carlos and sons have met with me for an annual schedule of pruning in the winter, flowering of the vines in the spring, leaf thinning, mowing, and mulching in the summer, and harvest in the fall," David describes.

"And that's the firm doing the harvest right now?" I ask.

"Yes, we have a contract with them, and I recommend keeping it with them. It will make it easier for both of you," David explains.

"Well, thanks for all of that, David. I know so much more about Ramey Winery than I did before today, and I have some ideas I'll talk to Tony about."

37

TONY COMES HOME after a long day of crushing.

"How are you?" I ask.

"The Sangiovese is done. Adam's thrilled. How was your day?" Tony asks.

"My day was fabulous. I learned so much that I have to share with you. Let's go out to dinner, and we can talk. There are no more grapes until next week, and maybe we can go to see your parents in a few days," I say.

"OK. We can go to Willie's Seafood for some oysters. I'm so excited to tell you everything I learned. Let's go now."

We walk into the restaurant and get seated. This place is only ten minutes from the winery. It will probably become our favorite.

"So, first, you need to see the property map on the conference room wall. It really helps put things into perspective. Next, I think we should terminate the lease of Southerly's. They need a thirty-day notice, and we should talk to Bertelli's Italian Deli about operating here," I share.

"I think that's a great idea. They can even sell our wine at their deli," Tony says. We can ask my cousin Francesca if they're interested."

"David said they use Sonoma Distributing to sell the wine to retail, restaurants, and bars. I can set up a meeting with them to review the current distribution list. It should be interesting. After that, we can decide to keep them or not," I explain.

Drinks and fried calamari arrive at the table. "It sounds like you had a full day," Tony says.

"I did, and I still have more to share. It sounds like the tasting room is under control. I need to meet Mary, the accountant, webmaster, marketer, and special events coordinator. I'd be surprised if she fills all those roles successfully. We may need to look at that. Before we do anything, I'll look at the books, tax returns, and current contracts to get a feel for the current financial state. However, the one thing we must do right after closing is transfer the license to us," I explain.

Dinner is served, and more wine is poured. "I'm impressed," Tony says. "You sound completely into it. I love it. You are investigating the kind of stuff that I can't do myself, so it sounds like we'll make a great team running this joint."

I look into Tony's baby blues and smile. I can hardly believe this is happening—what a dream. We would never be able to do this on our own without Uncle Luca.

"So, did you think about the name?" I ask.

"Yes, I have, but I forgot to tell you. I talked to Uncle Luca a few days ago. He said he discussed the name change of the winery with David, and that was a term of the agreement and sale; the name will be changed to CalaLuca," Tony says.

I smile at the sound of that. Uncle Luca, that is what this place is, and we can make it be that.

"Well, that means there will be many more business issues to deal with a name change, but I'm up for it. There will be more marketing and a new website and logo. That will allow us to truly make this place a Bertelli tradition. Let's go to East Marin in a few days. We can bring home more stuff, go to the restaurant and see your parents, the yacht club, and meet with Francesca about the deal.

We head south the next day to catch up with Maria and Vinnie. We go directly to the restaurant. Tony called and said we were on our way, so they were there. It's been a few weeks, and they are always excited to see us. We walk into the restaurant, and they appear out of nowhere. It isn't very crowded. Happy Hour is still an hour away. We get huge hugs and a seat at Tony's favorite table.

Everyone sits, and Vinnie says, "Tell us what is going on. Do you like working there? Is the harvest working you too hard? Do you like living there?"

"Calm down," Tony says. "The harvest is busy but OK. I'm working on crushing the grapes. Lolly is learning the other side of the business. We have a few things to talk to you about."

We all sit and relax, finally. It takes about an hour to drive from the winery to the restaurant, and we are just glad to be here. Tony gets up and goes into the back to order dinner for us. Maria asks, "So, are you enjoying the winery?"

"It's unbelievable. You can hardly call working there working. I've learned a lot about the business, and we need to talk to you about a few things."

Tony is back, and I'm ready to start talking, but Tony steps in. "We are ready to change the name of the winery to CalaLuca. That's OK with you two, right?" Tony asks.

Wine is delivered, and fried calamari for an appetizer.

"We're fine with it," Vinnie says.

"The other thing we are thinking of doing is bringing Bertelli's Italian Deli to the table and providing lunch at the venue. It will just grow their market tenfold and make the Bertelli family tradition shine."

We leave the restaurant and head to the East Marin Yacht Club. We arrive at the bar and sit at my favorite spot. Tony sits next to me.

Charles approaches us and says, "Hi, what are you two doing here? I thought you owned a winery in Sonoma and didn't mix with our type anymore."

"No, that's not true. We're the same people, but the opportunities that lie ahead for all of us are fantastic," I smile.

"Can I get you two something to drink?" Charles asks.

"We'll just take a bottle of the Zinfandel," Tony says.

When Charles returns with two glasses and a bottle, I say, "Do you have a minute? We have something to ask you."

"How's it going anyway?" Charles asks.

"Harvest is going full steam ahead, and there are a lot of other business things we need to take care of, which is why we're here," Tony says.

"We are changing the winery's name from Ramey to CalaLuca, the winery in Tuscany. Uncle Luca bought the winery to carry on his tradition here through us. I wanted to know if you would like to design a logo for us. It can be original and fresh, but it must embody tradition. If you are interested—and we'll pay you for your work, you should come to visit the vineyard and winery to get a feel for it, the same feel we've been getting the last few weeks," I explain and take a sip of wine.

"I would love to help you guys out," Charles says. "I think it's a great idea to visit the property. However, I work on weekends, so we'd have to plan for a weekday visit."

"You can submit a proposal to us and suggest the price. We are unfamiliar with this kind of thing," I add.

"Thanks, Charles," Tony says. "I like that you are helping us out. This will be a family thing, and you're like family to Lolly."

"How about you visit next Tuesday around 11:00 a.m.?" I ask. "I will send directions."

"That will work," Charles says.

Tony and I leave the yacht club and head to Bertelli's Italian Deli. Tony talked to his cousin Francesca and told her we would be on our way. We walk into the deli. This place is fabulous. It smells of garlic, salami, fresh bread, cheese, pasta, and sauces. Tony spots Francesca in the corner, and she motions us over to her. We walk over to her. Tony hugs her and introduces us.

"I'm so excited for you two. It's not every day you inherit a winery from an uncle. It must feel unreal for you," Francesca says.

"It's pretty unreal, but this is about the family; this isn't about us, which is why we are here. We want Bertelli's Italian Deli to take over the food service lease at the winery.

We can talk about the terms of the lease, but the bottom line is it's a great venue for you to expand your business," Tony explains.

"I'm very interested," Francesca says.

"I would suggest that you schedule a visit to CalaLuca in the next week, and we can come to terms of the lease," Tony says.

We head back to East Marin and drive to the triplex.

"Can we just sit here and look at the view? I need this, but it has been a very productive day," I smile. "And we will stay here tonight. That's ok, right?" I ask.

"I think this would be a great spot to land when we make it back down from the winery," Tony says.

"The rent's not that much, and it has a better view than your place," I say. "I just hope we can afford it. I quit my job and have no income."

"We'll be able to afford it. I'll give up my apartment, and we can use this when we come to see Maria and Vinnie."

"I would like to pack more stuff to haul up to CalaLuca," I say.

"That is fine," Tony says. "We'll keep chipping away at moving."

"I should have invited Cal and T down. I'll call right now."

Minutes later, the doorbell rings, and we open the front door. T and Cal walk in and hug everybody. I don't have much to eat since we haven't been here for weeks. However, we do have wine, and I can open something for the occasion. We open a Primitivo, and all sit around the table.

"We just drove down from Healdsburg today and went to the yacht club, met with Charles, and met with Tony's cousin Francesca, and now we are here with you," I say.

"So, how's it going?" T asks.

"It's an amazing ride. For us to live there, work there, try to get acclimated to the business side of things, work the harvest, and the property will close within a week; it's been surreal," I say. "I would like to invite you both to visit the winery, which will now be called CalaLuca Winery."

"I'd love to visit next week. I don't have any meetings or travel. Would that work for you?" T asks.

"I'll be crushing the Primitivo, which you can watch if you're there. Charles is coming on Tuesday if you want to be there at the same time as him. It's up to you; just let us know," Tony says.

"Cal said he is working at a winery in Sonoma. They are renovating the technology behind everything. It's an interesting business. You two must be thrilled."

"We are, Cal. We have only been here two-and-a-half weeks, and it's very overwhelming. We're moving to the property. We quit our jobs, but we will keep renting the triplex for when we come down to visit family, and you two and Charles fall into that category. See you next week."

38

DAVID KNOCKS ON the door at the small house we are staying in. Tony answers the door and sees David standing there.

"Hi, I'm here to tell you the property has closed. I will be moving out by the end of the day tomorrow. I will have the house cleaned the next day. Then, you two can move in," David says. "I have keys for you to everything, including the ATV. I'll leave them in the office, and the ATV will be parked out front."

"Thank you. We probably won't move in for a week or two, maybe after harvest. We're fine where we are," Tony says.

"I also have forwarding numbers and addresses for me. I'm not going far away. Call if you need anything," David says.

"It must be very emotional for you to leave this property after so many years. You're more than welcome to be here anytime. We'd love the old boss's critique of what we come up with over the next few weeks," Tony says.

The harvest of the Primitivo has been delayed for a few days so we can concentrate on the lease for the food service, the logo for the name change, and all the other things that go along with that.

I scheduled a meeting with Sonoma Distributing. They'll be here tomorrow. I grab their agreement and try to learn what they did for Ramey. According to the agreement, Sonoma works with Oliver's Markets, Willies Sea Food, Cattlemen's restaurants, Safeway grocery stores, and Total Wine and More.

"What kind of distribution are you thinking about?" I ask.

"I don't know. I'm just unfamiliar with that part of the business," Tony admits.

"I don't understand it either, but I don't think it makes sense for the distributing company to dictate your sales."

"You must have to negotiate a price for the distributor to buy at, and they can sell for what they want, whether it's to restaurants or grocery stores," Tony says.

"Maybe I can meet with Mary today and learn more about the financial side," I say.

"That would be great, Lolly. I will go to the city office to transfer our license now that we are closed on the property. Then, I'll head to our office. I can meet you there around 2:00 p.m.," Tony says.

"I should give Southerly's thirty-day notice today now that we talked to Francesca," I say.

"Good, Lolly. See you later this afternoon."

I walk down to the tasting room and office and look around for Mary. I finally find her. She looks at me and says, "Can I help you?"

"Yes, are you Mary?"

"Yes, I am. Who are you?" Mary asks.

"My name is Lolly, and Tony and I are the new owners of the winery," I explain. "How are you? I would like to meet with you if you have time to discuss what you do here. Is today a good time?" I ask.

"Now is fine. Come back to my office and have a seat. Can I get you a cup of coffee or water?" Mary asks.

"Actually, I'd love a cup of coffee, black, thanks," I say.

Mary returns with a cup for each of us. She sits behind her desk, takes a sip of coffee, and says, "Where do you want to start?"

"We can start with the financial statements and income taxes. I don't have a good feel for how much money the winery makes, how much they pay in taxes, and what the payroll is," I admit.

"Let me pull out last year's financial statement. We had a profit of $543,000. We paid $27,900 in property taxes and $357,000 in payroll for our six employees. Sales for the year was $2,324,900 for direct and distributed sales," Mary explains. "Expenses are $1.4 million. They include the bottles, labels, marketing and advertising, and any distributor and local event costs, such as the harvest fair," Mary explains.

"Well, that gives me a fine picture of where the winery has been. Tony will have to look through everything we went through today, but there are a few other things I wanted to talk to you about. You are responsible for the website, correct?" I ask.

"Yes, it doesn't take much maintenance," Mary says.

"Well, we are going to change the name, so you need to think of everything that will be required because of the name change. We are changing the name to CalaLuca. The whole website needs upgrading. So, let's talk a little about marketing. What are your responsibilities regarding marketing?" I ask.

"I maintain the winery membership in the local rotary club and make sure the winery is represented in the local wine competitions. We don't usually advertise. However, a request will come in occasionally, and we'll go for it," Mary explains.

"So, what about special events?" I ask.

'Well, we don't do special events very often—or at all," Mary says.

"I remember David telling me there was a barn on the property," I say.

"Yes, there is an old barn out in the far corner of the vineyard. We had one wedding there, and it was a disaster. The logistics were not there. The plans to get people in and out were a mess, and getting the barn in shape for the event never really happened," Mary says.

"But that doesn't mean that it's not something to consider in the future," I respond.

"Absolutely not," Mary says.

"So, I have one other question for you. Do you still want to work here for Tony and me?"

"I would like to keep my job and work for you," Mary admitted. "I love working here."

"From what we talked about today, I would be fine with you staying on with us. I can maybe hire you some help with the overload of stuff that will have to be done because of the name change," I explain.

Tony walks in, license in hand, and I run to give him a hug. "We'll have to frame that for the office," I say.

"Let's go to the tasting room bar and talk to Robert."

We walk through the office and end up in the tasting room. There are customers, and Robert is tending to their needs. He acknowledges our arrival, but we know he has to seal the deal with these people. It isn't long before they leave, a few bottles of wine in hand, and Robert brings two glasses to us.

"Hi, Robert," Tony says. "We thought we'd sit and chat since the property closed today, and David is moving out tomorrow."

"Thanks for letting me know," Robert says.

"Were you and David close?" Tony asks.

"I worked for him for twelve years. We had a great working relationship but very little personal relationship," Robert explains.

"Well, I'll just come right out and ask if you want to work for Lolly and me. We are making a few changes. Part of the deal in selling the property is changing the name of the winery to CalaLuca. The other big change is the food service lease will change to Bertelli's Italian Deli. We already gave Southerly's notice. They will be out soon," Tony says.

"So, how about you do a wine tasting for us just as you would if we walked off the street," I say.

Robert is ready to start his production. Tony and I sit in anticipation of the sale. That is what he's supposed to do while in the tasting room—sell wine.

"Our first taste is a Sangiovese. The grapes are grown right here on our property. The fruit is very forward and sweet." Robert pours two glasses for us. We pick up our glasses, swirl the wine around, and take a sip.

"I like this," I say.

Tony takes another sip and says, "So do I."

Robert returns with the Primitivo. We are waiting for his presentation. "This is a grape that is also grown on this property. It's fairly young for us but has a tremendous history in Italy," Robert smiles. He pours us a taste. We swirl, sniff, and taste. "Perfect. I like this one the best." Tony agrees.

Robert returns with his last taste of the day, a Syrah. "This Syrah is harvested in Dry Creek Valley, crushed here at the property, and has an amazing color that will blow the other crops away." Robert pours us a taste. We both taste and smile. Robert looks at us and realizes that he is on an interview to keep his job here. We don't want Robert to go anywhere. We need him here and would like to get to know him.

"So, can we talk about inventory, Robert?" Tony asks.

"Yes, what do you want to know?" Robert asks.

"Where is the wine that's for sale stored? Tony asks.

"It's stored here in this building. We can go take a look in a minute," Robert says.

"How do you keep track of what you have? I mean, once you sell out, that's it until next year, right?" Tony asks.

"The software we have connects our direct sales to our inventory, so we know what we have here on site," Robert explains. Tony and Robert walk to the storage room to see what Robert's talking about. There must be 200 cases of wine, and hopefully, there is some way to locate them in this room.

"Thanks for the tasting and the information, Robert."

Tony and I jump in the ATV and drive home. Tony is going to cook dinner tonight.

39

TONY DECIDED TODAY was the day to venture over to our new house. David has moved out and got the place cleaned. I picked the keys up from the office, and he's ready to go check it out. We both jump in the ATV and drive to the main residence. The views of the vineyard around the house are spectacular. Even the views farther through Sonoma County are fabulous. I don't know what to expect in the house; maybe I need to keep my expectations low. We have never been inside this house. I don't know what to expect.

We park the ATV and walk to the house. I get the keys and open the door. We walk in together and look around. We walk into a great room with huge ceilings and windows everywhere. The views from inside the house are better than the views outside. Tony looks at me. I hug him. This place is unbelievable. We walk to the kitchen and can't believe how upgraded it is. *OK, this has exceeded my expectations.* We wander upstairs to the master suite and the other bedrooms. I grab Tony by the arm and say, "Seriously, this is where we get to live?"

Tony walks to me, hugs me, and says, "This is our new home. I'm glad you like it."

"I love it! I don't know what to say. I just never experienced anything like this in my life. No one ever gave me anything.

Headquarters

I always had to work very hard for everything, but to have something like this be given to us, I feel so grateful that Uncle Luca would even do this for us. You must have worked wonders in Tuscany. We need to call and talk to Uncle Luca."

Tony calls Luca, and Luca answers the phone.

"So, how has the vineyard and winery treated you?" Luca asks.

"Uncle Luca, you can't believe how incredible this has been. David moved out two days ago. We had four days of crush and will have many more. The house is wonderful. The employees Robert and Mary are staying on board. We are going to change the name to CalaLuca, and Bertelli's Italian Deli has agreed to lease the space here. We are very excited," Tony says.

"Is there anything I didn't do for you?" Luca says.

"I can't believe you even asked me that," Tony responds.

"You taught me the wine business, the wine-making process, and bought this fabulous property for us. Lolly, my family, and I are forever grateful."

Charles should be here at 11:00, and T and Cal will also be here. I told everyone to meet in the tasting room. Charles and Gail walk in and look around. I ran over to hug him. "Hi, welcome. You found the place. Sit down at the bar. Can I pour you both a taste of wine?" I ask.

"Sure," Gail says. "We have so many questions for you both."

As soon as she said that, Trisha and Cal walked into the tasting room and over to Charles and Gail. "This is like the East Marin Yacht Club North," Charles says.

"It's just a coincidence that you both showed up at the same time, but now, I just have to give one tour for all of you." I smile.

I pour everyone tastes of wine. Tony says, "So, Charles, thanks for agreeing to create the logo for CalaLuca. The existing logo for Ramey is very traditional. We may want to update the feel of what CalaLuca means to this land."

"Charles, I know you can come up with something," I say.

Everyone takes a taste of their wine. "Let's take a quick tour of the property and end up back here for lunch," I say.

We all jump in the ATV. Tony drives for a tour of the vineyards, the facilities, the residences, and then back to the tasting room.

We sit back in the tasting room and pour a Primitivo.

"Wow! This property, the vineyards, the facilities, the residences—it is phenomenal," T says.

"Thank you," Tony says. "We're very overwhelmed by the whole thing."

We go back to the patio to get lunch served, maybe for the last time, just as Francesca walks in the door. It should be interesting for her to experience what was here prior.

"Hi, you made it," Tony says. "Let me introduce you to everyone. This is Francesca. She manages the Bertelli Italian Deli, which will lease the food service here. This is Charles and Gail. Charles has been commissioned to create a new Logo for CalaLuca, and this is Trisha and Cal. They are great friends who just happen to be visiting here today."

"Nice to meet everyone. Have Vinnie and Maria been here?" Francesca asks.

"They were here a few weeks ago and were just as overwhelmed as we are."

I pour another taste of Syrah while everyone chats, and we get lunch started. The Italian Deli will be a fabulous addition to the wine experience.

Tony and I say goodbye to Charles, Gail, Trisha, and Cal so we can meet with Francesca. We come back to the tasting room. Francesca sits down and takes a sip of wine. Tony and I sit next to her.

"So, we need to come up with an agreeable lease structure that will accommodate you and the winery. Since this is new to us, I'm looking to you to come up with terms we both can live with," Tony says.

"I think the lease can be $5,000 monthly, and we can take over the daily food service. We will need an area for the refrigerators and display cases. The display cases usually sell the product. We can do something different here to give it a new twist."

"Let's go look at the options we have in the storage room and see what we can do."

40

TWO WEEKS PASS. Francesca mobilizes her staff, delivers the display cases, and sets up how they will function. The Primitivo harvest is complete, and I meet with Sonoma Distributing today. Francesca already asks about an office space, which is fine. She can help organize the whole area in the back.

The Sonoma Distributing truck pulls up in front of the tasting room. The driver hops out of the truck and walks in. He walks over to me and says, "I'm supposed to meet with the new owners."

"Hi, I'm Lolly. I'm the new owner, along with Tony Berrtelli. Let's go take a seat in the conference room. Do you want a taste of wine?" I ask.

"No, I'm working."

"How about a water?"

"That will be perfect."

I get a water, and we sit at the conference table. "Hi, I'm Lolly. What's your name?"

"Harvey."

"Harvey, I just have a few questions about your existing contract with Ramey and whether you want to move forward with us. Can I see the current distribution lists for the winery?" I ask. Harvey pulls out the existing list and hands it to me.

"It is very straightforward," Harvey says. "Bev Mo, Cattlemen's, Safeway, Bottle Barn, and Willie's Wet Bar. I'm here twice a month; payment is due at the time of pickup."

"How is your price for our wine determined?" I ask.

"It is mutually determined before signing the contract, along with quantity and variety," Harvey explains.

"We are changing the name to CalaLuca Winery. Are you OK with that?" I ask. "We would like to add Bertelli's Restaurant and Bertelli's Italian Deli in Larkspur to the distribution list. I want you to meet Francesca, who will run the food service. She may have other needs for you to bring to them. Let me go get her and ask her to join us."

I go back to the office and ask Francesca to join us. We return to the conference room, "Harvey, this is Francesca. Francesca, Harvey," I say.

"Nice to see you, Harvey," Francesca says.

"You two know each other?" I ask.

"I've worked with Sonoma Distributing for many years, and Harvey is the man," Francesca smiles.

"This is great news. Why don't you two talk about what changes to the contract will be necessary? That is, of course, if Harvey wants to continue working with CalaLuca," I say.

"I'll be in my office if either of you have any questions. It was nice meeting you, Harvey," I smile as I walk away.

I make my way to Mary's office and knock on the door. "Come in, please, sit down. How are you, Lolly?" Mary asks.

"I'm still a little overwhelmed, but your and Robert's help has made things much easier. Have you met Francesca?" I ask.

"No," Mary says.

"Maybe later today, I can introduce her to you and Robert, and she can have a taste of wine," I suggest.

"Mary, I've been thinking about having a harvest party in a few weeks," I continue. "I'm thinking live music, an open house with friends and family, and a formal announcement of the CalaLuca brand. Pulling it off will be a lot of work, so I wanted to talk to you first. We can talk to Francesca later about this, too. I think she will be a vital part of our success. She is family, not just a company leasing the space. She will have responsibilities here to help Tony and I manage the business."

"I like the thought of that," Mary replies.

Tony shows up at the office an hour later.

"How did harvest go?" I ask.

"We had seventeen tons of grapes today, and Adam was very pleased," Tony shares.

"Well, I'd like to get everyone together in an hour or so to introduce them to Francesca and let's get Adam down here before he goes home. Can you arrange that?" I ask.

"I think that will be great. I'll call Adam right now," Tony says.

"I call Robert to grab a few open bottles in the tasting room for us to enjoy and tell Mary and Francesca to meet us on the patio at 4:00 p.m."

Tony and I sit back and relax. "I met with Harvey with Sonoma Distributing today, and it ends up that Francesca knows Harvey. I would like to talk about giving Francesca the responsibility of managing Sonoma Distributing and the inventory, which is directly related to the sales. She knows much more about this than we do. We can pay her a salary for her services if that's OK with you and her. We can talk about it briefly if you'd like."

We go to the patio, and Robert follows us out with glasses and wine bottles in hand. Soon, Mary, Adam, and Francesca show up.

"Hi, thanks for coming. Let me quickly introduce everyone. Starting here, we have Adam, our winemaker; Francesca, our food service manager; Mary, our accountant; and Robert, our tasting room host. We are trying to get organized, and all of you have helped tremendously. Robert, can you pour a taste for everyone while I continue?

"We are coming up on our name change, which will be dramatic. My idea is to have a harvest celebration to celebrate the end of the harvest and announce the official name change. I envision live music, food, and gift wine glasses with the new logo to introduce us to the neighborhood. What do you think?"

"Harvest still has another week," Adam says.

"We can pick a date for this to happen right now," I explain. "Does anyone have an opinion about when the party should be?" I ask.

"I need to make sure my company is ready to perform," Francesca says.

"I need to notify the appropriate news advertising spots of the event," Mary says.

"Can you add to your to-do list to book the live music and order 300 wine glasses and fifty golf shirts with the new logo? The staff can purchase the new shirts. I'll help you with the details," I explain.

"I need to request additional tasting room staff because I could not handle that size crowd alone."

"Wow, this has been successful already. We have two things that will dictate the celebration date—the end of harvest and finalizing the logo. I will communicate any updates with all of you soon," I say.

41

TODAY IS MOVING day, and we are heading to East Marin to pick up a few of my things and stop in at the yacht club to see if Charles has anything to show us. Then, it's off to Tony's place to pick up a few of his things, and finally, we get to eat dinner with Maria and Vinnie. It will be nice to be next to the bay. I think we'll probably do this every few weeks. Not moving, but just visiting the bay.

My place looks fine for somewhere that isn't being lived in. I get a suitcase and quickly pack the rest of my things. I turn to Tony and say, "This will be the perfect spot to escape from the winery. Do you agree?"

"I do. This place puts my place to shame," Tony says. We just need to budget for it in the business plan.

"Well, I'm ready. Let's go see how Charles is doing. Tony carries my suitcase to the car, and I lock up and make my way to the car. We drive to the yacht club, walk into the bar, and see Charles staring at us. "What are you two doing here?" Charles asks.

"We're members here, remember. We were in town and wondered if you had any inspirations for the logo to show us," I explain.

"As a matter of fact, your timing could not have been better. I was just putting the finishing touches on my drafts for you to look at. Sit down. What can I get you to drink?" Charles asks.

"I'll have a red zin," I say.

"I'll have a draft beer," Tony says.

Charles delivers the drinks and disappears into the back room for a while. He returns with his sketchbook and looks at us like he's excited about what he has to show us. He sits down and turns to his first draft. It says "CalaLuca" in a thin white font on a purple bunch of grapes.

"I like it. I can imagine this on wine bottles, signage, and advertising. What about you, Tony?" I ask.

"I like it but want to see what else he has."

Charles turns the page of his sketchbook. He has a landscape of the view from the patio with a sculpture of the word "CalaLuca" in the meadow.

"I like the sculpture," Tony smiles.

"Maybe we need to make that sculpture and put it in the meadow," I say, "and photograph that for the logo without the landscape view. What do you think, Charles?"

"I'm just listening. I have one more to show you."

Charles again turns the page of his sketchbook. We see a California License Plate with "CalaLuca" on it and a license plate surround that says: "I'd rather be wine tasting."

"Oh my, I love them all," I smile at Charles. "They all have such different feelings to them. I like seeing California on the last one. Uncle Luca will like that. That one is also whimsical, light, and fun."

"I like it, too. I can see that as a bottle label, on stationary, signage, all of it," Tony explains. "Great job, Charles. How much do we owe you?"

"That's entirely up to you," Charles says.

"How about $2,000? I would like to run this by Maria, Vinnie, and Francesca. Can I write you a check?" Tony asks.

"Certainly. Would you two like another round?"

"Yes, please, and maybe we can discuss the next steps and graphic artists you might recommend. This isn't our area of expertise," I explain.

After Charles shares some of his contacts with us, we finish our drinks, say our goodbyes, and head over to Tony's to pick up the last of his things. The rent expires in two days.

He has most of his stuff at the winery, but we need to make one final check. Then, it's off to Bertelli's for a short meeting with Maria and Vinnie and dinner.

Charles made us copies of his drafts to show Maria and Vinnie. We walk into the restaurant and right to Tony's favorite table, holding our draft logos. Maria and Vinnie make their way to the dining room and rush over to greet us. It's been a few weeks.

"Welcome, come sit down," Maria says. Tony and I exchange hugs with them and sit down. We were anxious to show them the logo drafts. Tony pulls out a Ramey Primitivo and sends it to the back for opening and pouring.

"We have some drafts of the new logo for the winery for you to look at. I think we made our decision, but we would love your opinions," Tony says.

Alfredo arrives at the table with the wine and glasses, pours everyone a sip, and disappears.

"So, do you want to start with the one we like or do it like we did and randomly go through them?" Tony asks.

Maria says, "Just show us what you like."

"I agree," Vinnie says.

Tony takes a sip of wine, gets the file out, and shares the California license plate design with them. "This one is fun, whimsical, and not as formal as Ramey's logo. What do you think?"

"I like it," Maria says. "I think fun is better than traditional for you two. You have to create the future of this winery, so this is the first step."

"I agree," Vinnie says. "Your youth has to be reflected in the winery from now on. I think that was Uncle Luca's intent."

I look at Tony, and he looks at me, both of us shocked at how wonderful that all sounds.

"Cheers," Tony says, "Here's to CalaLuca Winery."

We all lift our glasses right as dinner arrives.

"We do have one more thing to talk about. We are planning a harvest celebration to celebrate harvest completion and introduce the name change, us, and Bertelli Italian Deli. We plan to have the logo complete as well," Tony explains. "You can stay in your new space at the vineyard after."

"When will it be?" Maria asks.

"To pull this off, we'll probably need about a month for it to all come together. We'll let you know what day we decide," Tony says. "Now, we can go back to eating."

42

A MONTH GOES by. The Syrah is harvested. Francesca has moved her business in and has already made an impact. The new logo was created and being distributed. The harvest celebration is two weeks out. We will announce our name change and feature Bertelli's Italian Deli with samples of what is available for purchase in the wine-tasting room. We covered the wine labels of the existing wine to promote the new logo. We ordered 300 wine glasses with the new logo to give to all the event patrons. The string quartet will provide some background music. Invitations go out to family and friends for the harvest celebration. Mary has posted an advertisement about the celebration with the new logo and offerings. Robert is working with a catering service to help us on that day. I'm sure Francesca can use some supplemental help for the sampling area. I use the contacts that Charles provided to make banners to hang above the entry to the winery and above the tasting room for the event. The meadow will be a tasting area, sampling olives, salami, pickles, and wine for purchase in the tasting room.

Tony and I meet with the staff at 3:00 p.m. to discuss this. It feels like we're planning a wedding. Robert sets us up nicely on the patio, and the meeting begins.

"Robert, how are the negations with the caterer going? Do you need help? Maybe Francesca or I can help," I say.

"I can use the help. I don't know the staffing requirements of the sample tables. Maybe the three of us can meet right after the meeting and quickly discuss the specifics," Robert says.

"Perfect. Thanks, Robert. Mary, what do you need from any of us?" I ask. "And what else do you have remaining to do?"

"Well, I still need to confirm with the rental company the number of tables with tablecloths and chairs we need and the delivery time," Mary says. "The glasses and shirts arrived yesterday."

"I will help you with that. What time for the event did you include on the invitations and announcements?" I ask.

"11:00 a.m. to 3:00 p.m.," Mary says.

"An 8:00 a.m. delivery time will give us enough time before the event begins. Will the rental company do the set-up, tablecloths and all?" I ask.

"I can ask them," Mary responds.

"We need them to include that in their pricing because we don't have the staff to do it—and take down. Include that in their price, as well," I say to Mary. "Anything else?"

"Not for right now, but I would like to meet again before the event to make sure we're on track," Mary states.

"Great suggestion. I'll let everyone know when," I say. "Francesca, what do you need? You already hired catering help and rental stuff, correct? What else?"

"We need to come up with a sampling menu so I can make sure we have the inventory to back it up," Francesca says.

"I'll help you with that," Tony says.

"Thanks, Tony," Francesca smiles. "This seems like it's going to work out just right for us."

"I'm glad," Tony smiles.

"OK, Adam, let's talk about tours of the wine-making facility. Should we try to do it or not? Maybe we should just have you work in the tasting room and promote the wine sales that way. What do you think?" I ask.

"It sounds like it will be busy and crowded, and maybe me stationed in the tasting room would make more sense for such an event," Adam states.

"I agree," Tony says. "Now all we have to do is devise a parking plan. The meadow will be full of food and drinks. Adam, do you have any thoughts on an area for overflow parking?"

"Actually, I do. The area adjacent to the wine facility is a direct route from the entrance. We could reroute traffic from the main parking lot to that location if we need to," Adam explains.

"Excellent, Adam. Now, we have to figure out the logistics of traffic control. Do we need to hire someone?" Tony says.

"Actually, a parking attendant would be someone to consider."

"Mary, can you help with this?" I ask.

"Absolutely," Mary says. "I'll let you know."

"So, I think we are good for now. If Robert and Francesca can stay for five minutes, that would be helpful. Regarding manpower, if you two thought of what you could anticipate, Robert, what would it be? How many more workers will you need?" I ask.

"If we're pouring on the tables in the meadow, I would need a person at every station. Do we know how many wine stations we will have?" Robert asks.

"We can determine that right now. We want to feature our three varieties of wine," I say. "Actually, I have an idea. What if we buy three six-foot tables? We will always be able to use them. One will be for the wine glasses to give to guests on their way in. The other two can be in the meadow, one for wine and the other for samples. That could limit the staff to four, at the most."

"Bertelli's Italian Deli needs the sampling menu," Francesca says.

"OK, let's decide what to sample," I say.

Francesca starts with her ideas—olives, salami, pickles, bread, and two different kinds of cheese.

"That would be fine. Will that fit on a six-foot table?" I ask. "There will be samples in the winery as well."

"I think that will be fine," Francesca says.

"So, based on that, we need twelve tables and tablecloths and six chairs at each for seating," I say. "If you and Adam are stationed in the tasting room, Robert and the catering staff can be in the meadow. Mary can restock and tidy up during the event."

Tony and I walk away and get into the ATV, and head home. We walk into the main house, and it all still feels like a dream.

43

IT'S HERE—THE HARVEST celebration. We can't wait for our friends and family to join us today to celebrate so many things. It's been a busy morning getting everything in place. The string quartet arrived; the staff had their new shirts on, and everyone was in their positions. Tony and I are ready to be at the forefront to greet our family, friends, and patrons.

Everything seems to be going as planned.

Tony and I stand in front of the table full of gift wine glasses. The first to greet us are Maria and Vinnie. Tony makes sure they are escorted to their cottage.

"Hi, Maria. Hi Vinnie," I say. "Take a wine glass for your tasting today." They smile and move on.

Next, Charles and Gail come to enjoy the party.

"Welcome, you two. Take a wine glass to taste."

Dozens of local patrons arrive, receive their glasses, and move to the meadow.

Hank Evans comes to the table with Denise right behind him. "It looks like you survived the layoff," Hank says.

"I don't need no stinking job at H&S. We'll talk later," I say, handing him a glass. "Thanks for coming."

Denise follows right behind Hank.

"Thanks for coming. Take a wine glass. Sorry, we don't have any brandy," I say.

Cal and Trisha walk in, and she smiles.

"Take a wine glass and enjoy," I say.

I see Barry Bailey approaching the table, and he says, "So, this is why you quit your job at Beevis, Inc.?"

"This beats downtown Oakland," I say. "Thanks for joining us. Take a wine glass for tasting, and enjoy the samples from the deli."

Jose smiles as he approaches the table.

"It looks as if you did OK after being laid off from H&S," Jose says.

"I didn't have to quit, which is what I did at Beevis, Inc. Barry is here, somewhere, and he hired me; thanks to you for reaching out to him to let him know I would be calling him. Take a wine glass, and enjoy your stay," I say.

David Ramey walks up to Tony and me. "I'm so proud of what you two did to this place."

"Hi, David," Tony says. "I'm glad you could make the celebration. Behind him, a man says hi to David and comes up to Tony and me. "Hi, I'm the Mayor of Healdsburg. My name is Harry White."

"Oh my, what an honor to meet you. We are committed to this community and support everything local. Thank you for attending. Here's a wine glass for tasting and enjoy," Tony says.

Just in time, the Bertelli cousins wander to the table for their wine glasses. We direct them to the meadow or the tasting room for a taste of wine. Most of them have already sampled the deli's specialties.

The celebration is a tremendous success. Tony moves closer to say he needs to bring everyone together for an announcement.

Tony asks if everyone in the tasting room can come out and everyone in the meadow can look at him. He asks the string quartet to take a break, saying we have an announcement that we would like to deliver.

"Can everyone make sure they have a sip of wine to participate in the grand toast?" Tony announces. "I'll wait a few minutes to let that happen."

Tony turns to me, smiles, and whispers, "This couldn't have turned out any better," and hugs me.

"Welcome to CalaLuca Winery. Thank you, everyone, for celebrating this amazing winery and vineyard today. I had the fortune of coming into this property by an Uncle in Italy who purchased this winery from David Ramey. David is here today, and I couldn't be more pleased to follow in his footsteps. I would like everyone to raise their wine glasses to a grand toast. Here's to Uncle Luca; God bless you and thank you for giving Lolly and me this wonderful property and business. Cheers!" We toast. "Lolly and I couldn't be more grateful to be the owners of this property, and with that, I do have one last request. LORETTA 'LOLLY' NOVAK, WILL YOU MARRY ME!"

THE END

ABOUT THE AUTHOR

C. Atkinson derived her pen name from her given name, Charlene, her nickname Cricket, and her maiden name, Chopnak. Born and raised in a suburb of Pittsburgh, PA, she attended the University of Pittsburgh and received a degree in civil engineering. She was recruited out of college at a major construction company in San Francisco. She lives in Penngrove, CA, with her husband, Kerry, and her cat, Mango.

Made in the USA
Las Vegas, NV
27 March 2024